'You're delic‍ KU-593-210
her again. 'I want to eat you.'

Tessa was weak but she fought. 'No.'

'Why not?' He kissed her again, or she kissed him—she couldn't tell which, only that it was glorious and she revelled in it.

'Because. . .just because. I thought you were playing. Pretending.'

'I never pretend.'

Suddenly she heard the adult male intent in his voice and she stiffened, then carefully pulled herself away, realising she'd underestimated his seriousness. 'James. . .no.'

'But I want you,' he calmly replied.

A New Zealand doctor with restless feet, **Helen Shelton** has lived and worked in Britain and travelled extensively. Married to an Australian she met while on safari in Africa, she recently moved to Sydney where they plan to settle for a little while at least. She has always been an enthusiastic reader and writer and inspiration for the background for her medical romances comes directly from her own experiences working in hospitals in several countries around the world.

Recent titles by the same author:

POPPY'S PASSION

A SURGEON'S SEARCH

BY
HELEN SHELTON

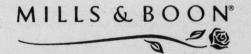

MILLS & BOON®

*First published in Great Britain 1997
Harlequin Mills & Boon Limited,
Eton House, 18-24 Paradise Road, Richmond, Surrey TW9 1SR*

© Helen Shelton 1997

ISBN 0 263 80520 4

*Set in Times 10 on 10½ pt. by
Rowland Phototypesetting Limited
Bury St Edmunds, Suffolk*

03-9801-53543-D

*Printed and bound in Great Britain
by Mackays of Chatham PLC, Chatham*

CHAPTER ONE

TRAFFIC at Swiss Cottage was hell.

Stuck in the jam with buses in front of him and beside him coughing black smoke into the hot afternoon, James raised the window of his BMW and switched the air-conditioning to high. He drummed his fingers impatiently on the steering-wheel, then reached for his mobile to call his secretary.

'Lucy, it's me,' he said. 'I was late leaving the Free and I'm stuck in traffic. How many have you got?'

'Four waiting. Two to come.'

'Anything major?'

'Three varicose veins, one laparoscopic gall-bladder follow-up. And there's a woman here to see you—she's been here since twelve.' Lucy sounded irritated. 'She says you agreed to see her but she's not on the computer and I wasn't sure about whether to make up some notes. Her name's Mathesson. Tessa Mathesson.'

'Tessa. . .?' But then he stiffened as he remembered, startled that he could have forgotten.

'No notes,' he said abruptly. 'She's not a patient.'

In their exchange of letters weeks ago he'd suggested they met at his rooms because Wednesday was his quiet-est day—he usually managed a full sixty-minute break before his afternoon clinic. This week, though, hadn't been normal. A colleague at the Free was on leave and he'd covered his call overnight, and during the early hours of the morning he'd had to take two emergency admissions to Theatre.

'I'm going to be thirty minutes.' The bus ahead moved and he inched the BMW forward to catch it, then had to brake again when the flow stopped. 'Maybe more.' He shifted back into neutral. 'Offer everybody coffee. From what I remember, Tessa's flying out first thing in the morning so she's probably booked up the rest of the day.' He made up his mind quickly. 'If she can't wait ask her to let me know next time she's going to be in town.'

But then he frowned, realising that that was probably exactly what Tessa was expecting. She, with or without her husband, only managed to get to London every few years, and the last time they'd been in town he'd been too busy to see them as well.

And depositing a generous cheque into Tessa's charity's account hadn't exactly allayed his guilt about that, he acknowledged grimly. 'No, second thoughts,' he amended. 'See if she's already booked somewhere to stay tonight. If not, there's a set of house keys in my top drawer. But warn her I have to go back to the Free after this clinic and I'll be home late.'

There was a brief but frosty silence before Lucy said, 'Your keys?'

'My keys,' he confirmed. He put the car back into gear and edged forward again as the lights ahead turned briefly amber then green.

'Your house keys?' she demanded, managing to sound both incredulous and affronted.

James's mouth compressed 'That's right.' He wondered if Tessa could hear this conversation—if that was the reason for the unwarranted possessiveness clouding Lucy's tone.

Moderately efficient and blessed with the computer skills needed to organise his private practice, Lucy was valuable to him, he'd decided. But only as long as her peevishness about failing to entice him into deepening their relationship didn't interfere with her work or his patients.

The lights had turned red again with no more movement from the bus. Behind him someone hooted. 'Any mail?'

'The usual things,' Lucy said stiffly. 'Another request for you to talk at that Singapore conference, plus a dozen letters asking for reprints of your *Journal of Surgery* article last month.'

'Send them out.'

'And. . .I'll give this Tessa woman your keys, then,' she said slowly.

'Do that.' The bus was still stationary but the right lane had started to move and James snapped the phone shut, threw it aside and accelerated swiftly into the gap and across the intersection, ignoring the indignant blare from the horn of the car behind.

Lucy greeted him silkily when he arrived at his rooms. 'She's only just left.' Her carefully painted mouth formed itself into a pout. 'She'll meet you at your home.'

'Good.' Sparing her only a brief glance, James collected the files for his afternoon patients and opened the waiting-room door. 'Sorry I was delayed,' he said briskly, smiling at the waiting women. 'Lucy's looked after you, I hope. Have you all had coffee?'

'Yes, thank you.' They each returned his apologetic smile warmly and his first scheduled patient, Delia Buttrose-Allen—charity worker and wife of one of the richest industrialists in the country—beamed at him as she preceded him towards his office. 'That lovely young Dr Mathesson's been talking to us,' she explained.

'Oh, yes?' James rolled his eyes, wondering why he hadn't foreseen that. Letting Tessa loose in a room with four rich women probably hadn't been a good idea, at least not for his patients. 'How much did she extort from you?'

'Enough to keep that hospital of hers healthy a little longer,' Delia admitted dryly. 'You know we gave years ago to the war relief fund they set up for Sadakh but I thought the war ended when the Russians pulled out. I had no idea there was civil war now. Things sound worse than they've ever been out there.'

'That's right.' The mainstream press no longer publicised the war to any great extent but James couldn't help but know everything about the conflict in Sadakh. For the past five years he'd received a detailed report every quarter, all penned personally by Tessa. 'She's doing an amazing job.'

'She's an amazing woman.' Delia perched on his examination bench and began delicately winding down her stockings to show him the veins he'd operated on two months before. 'I'm going to arrange a fund-raising luncheon next time she's in London. There's a faint chance she'll be able to get away in another six months if we can make it worth her while. I'll finance her trip, of course. I imagine she's a passionate speaker so I don't think it'll be difficult to canvass more donations.'

'Of course she explained the Foreign Office isn't over-joyed at what she's doing?'

'Foreign Office, bah!' Delia waved a jewelled hand with the dismissiveness that came from extreme wealth. 'We don't have to take any notice of those stuffy geriatrics.'

James smiled. 'Still, they're part of Tessa's problem,' he explained, examining her legs from the top of her thighs down, pleased with the way she'd healed. 'She can't canvass too openly for funds—she has to be discreet.'

'We'll be very discreet.' Delia looked delighted and James realised that the suggestion of intrigue had prob-ably doubled her enthusiasm. 'So it's top secret, then?'

'Low profile's a better description.' He got her to stand, then crouched to inspect the results. 'They're much better, aren't they?'

'Superb.' Delia smiled down at her legs. 'Best they've looked in twenty years. You're marvellous, James. Best surgeon in Harley Street. We all know that.'

'Then you should have come to me in the first place,' he said easily. Part of his surgery had involved redoing work that had been done by someone else two years earlier.

'I would have if the waiting list to see you wasn't so

atrocious.' She refastened her stockings. 'Remember you refused to zoom me to the top.'

'Because varicose veins aren't an emergency,' he countered. 'At least, not in your case.'

'Allow me my little vanities,' she said briskly. 'Besides, the amount you charge me, I imagine I'm subsidising your entire list.' Then she collected her handbag and smiled at him. 'You know I can think of at least a dozen beautiful young things dying to meet London's second most eligible bachelor. So when are you coming to one of my functions?'

'Probably never,' he said dryly. 'But let me know well in advance if you are organising a luncheon for Tessa. I'll make that.'

'Good boy.' She looked pleased. 'With you there, we should double our attendance. Tessa will be pleased.' Her gaze turned thoughtful. 'She's a beautiful woman.'

'Isn't she?' James showed her to the door. 'Married, too.'

'Pity.' Delia's beautifully made-up eyes gleamed shrewdly. 'You've been a playboy too long.'

'Don't believe everything you read,' he said lightly, walking her past a glaring Lucy to the main door. 'I work too hard to have the social life I'm credited with.'

'From what I hear, you play hard, too.' She kissed his cheek, engulfing him briefly in the strong, expensive scent of her perfume. 'Thanks for everything, James. Send your outrageous bill to my secretary as usual.'

'Goodbye, Delia.' James shut the door firmly.

Lucy said, 'I hate it when people talk like that. You're not a playboy. Don't they understand the hours we work?'

We? James's mouth twitched. As far as he knew, Lucy worked strictly ten till six.

As soon as he'd finished seeing his private patients that afternoon James battled the traffic again to return to the Free. One of the men he'd operated on earlier that day, a twenty-four-year-old with massive abdominal injuries following a motorcycle accident, was stable but still being ventilated in the intensive care unit.

'His haemoglobin's stable at twelve but he's had thirty units of blood plus all the extras,' Tim, his registrar, explained. 'Oxygen levels are good.'

James checked the chart and then the catheter bag, pleased to note that the urine, earlier bloodstained, was clearing and dilute. 'Good amounts of urine.'

'His kidneys are managing OK.' The ICU registrar flicked through the notes, inspecting the test results. 'There was probably only thirty minutes when he didn't have a decent blood pressure so fingers crossed we've got away without any permanent damage to them.'

James pulled his stethoscope out of his pocket and listened to the man's abdomen, not surprised that it was still silent. Considering the degree of trauma sustained and the amount of bowel he'd had to remove, it would be unreasonable to expect the remaining bowel to begin functioning before the end of the week.

He noted the casts on his patient's left leg and arm. 'What are the orthopods up to?'

'The femur is fractured and they've pinned it,' he was told. 'And fixed the elbow. They're going to wait a few days for the swelling to reduce before tackling the facial fractures.'

'No signs of significant head injury?'

'CT scan this afternoon's normal.' His registrar shoved the scans up onto the X-ray box so he could look at them. 'We got the neurosurgery people in, just in case, but they're not worried.'

'Good.' James nodded at his junior approvingly. 'Well done. Looks like he's going to get through this.'

They went to see the other patient he'd operated on. Also still in the ICU and unconscious and ventilated, the seventy-year-old man was doing less well. Known to have diverticular disease, where the bowel formed little side pouches off the main cavity, he'd presented with severe abdominal pain and shock and had gone into cardiac arrest in Casualty. He'd been resuscitated but an X-ray had shown free air within his abdomen, signifying that part of the bowel had perforated.

James had operated immediately, removing the part of his bowel containing the diverticulum which had burst open and cleaning the area thoroughly and repeatedly, but their patient was still showing signs of septicaemia— blood poisoning—with fever, and low blood pressure and a racing pulse.

'Microbiology will have a preliminary result on the swabs by tonight,' his registrar told him, 'so we might be able to adjust the antibiotics to something more specific, but at the moment we think we're covering everything.'

James bent over the man's abdomen. There was very little coming out of the drains he'd placed. 'Urine?'

'Clear.' The ICU registrar passed him the result. 'Surprisingly.'

'How is he medically?' he asked.

'Cardiology say he's as fit as we could expect,' Tim said. 'They think the arrest was purely related to the septicaemia.'

'We might end up going back in.' James picked up the X-ray folder and shoved the latest chest X-ray up onto the box. Relatively clear, there was no sign there of another focus of infection. Which suggested there might still be a source of infection within the abdomen.

'Give him twenty-four hours of antibiotics,' James declared. 'CT scan the abdomen tomorrow morning to look for a collection, in case one's built up since we operated. If there's nothing we can drain through the skin. Still no improvement this time tomorrow then we'll open him up again and take another look.'

He washed his hands. 'I'd like to speak with his wife again. Is she still here?'

'In the relatives' room.' His registrar followed him. 'I've been very cautious.'

'At this stage that's wise.' James checked his watch.

It was after seven and he knew the younger man had been on duty since seven-thirty the morning before. Thirty-six busy hours on duty had been draining for both of them but, unlike his registrar, at least he'd been able to spend some time away from the hospital during those hours.

'Go home, Tim. We're in Theatre and then on call again tomorrow so you need your sleep. I'll speak to the on-call team—get them to call me direct if there're any problems overnight.'

'Thanks.' Tim grinned his appreciation wearily. 'We've five patients on each operating list for tomorrow so it'll be a long day. I thought we'd start with Mrs Dyer together. Is that OK?'

James nodded. Mrs Dyer had had a lot of surgery in the past. He was confident he'd be able to remove her bowel tumour, but with so many adhesions and scars from her previous surgery it wasn't going to be an easy procedure. Tim's help, as he was more experienced than either of his SHOs, would be useful.

When Tim had left James opened the door to the relatives' room and signalled for his patient's wife to come with him. 'He's holding steady,' he explained quietly, taking her into one of the offices where they could have more privacy. 'But not improving.'

Mrs Watkins's swollen eyes suggested that she'd done a lot of crying since he'd last spoken to her at lunchtime, but for now she seemed composed. 'I understand, Dr Hyatt. You're all doing your best. I understand.'

'The operation today should have cleaned out all the infection inside his abdomen but the blood still seems to be infected. Tomorrow we'll have a better idea what's going to happen—once the antibiotics have had more time to work.'

'They might not work—is that what you're saying, Doctor?'

'They might not.' James hated this—hated the uncertainty—but he knew it wasn't fair to be over-confident when he didn't feel it himself. 'We might need to operate again but that might not work either.'

'He—he wanted to go to Greece.' She gripped his hand tightly, her fingers icy cold. 'He always wanted to go to Greece. He studied it up at the polytechnic years ago. The culture, the ancient Greeks, the temples—he loves all of that. But we've never been. We usually go to Devon for the holidays and I was always frightened about going abroad and we were so busy, what with the grandchildren. . .' She looked up at him. 'I should have let him go. We both should have gone.'

James said, 'He looks as if he's had a contented life.'

'I think he's been happy.' She'd started to cry now. 'I've done my best. If he gets better I want to go with him to see Greece. Before we're old. What do you think?'

'I think you need some sleep,' he said quietly. 'Go home for a while. He's sedated so he won't wake tonight. But I'll ask the nurses to call you straight away if there's any change.'

'I do need to sleep,' she whispered. 'I can't think straight any more. Our daughter's coming up after supper. I'll wait until she comes and then I'll go and rest.'

After seeing her back to her husband's bed, James called at the ward to check the remainder of his admissions from the night before and to see the patients he'd be operating on the following day.

It was after eight by the time he made his way back to his BMW, and twenty minutes later that he drove up the drive of his Finchley home.

The door opened before he reached it. 'James,' Tessa squealed, launching herself at him from the top step. 'In the flesh. Finally. I can't believe it.'

Taken unawares, he dropped his briefcase and caught her, twirling her around as he smiled into her laughing face. 'Still the same shy, quiet little Tessa,' he teased. 'You look wonderful.'

And she did. With gleaming blonde hair cropped carelessly short, slim, tanned body in jeans and T-shirt and skin freckled and bare, she looked youthful and gorgeous. For a fraction of a second he felt himself responding to her vitality and he released her abruptly, startled by his reaction.

Grimly reminding himself that Tessa was a married woman, James stepped back.

Patently oblivious to the sensation that had left him suddenly wary, Tessa simply laughed again. 'James, you look terrific.' She fluttered her eyelashes at him, seeming totally and blissfully relaxed. 'Stunning, in fact. No wonder you're the darling of the jet set. It is you I keep reading about in all the gossip pages, isn't it?'

'Since when did you ever read gossip pages?' He retrieved his briefcase and shooed her ahead of him into the house. 'And stop bouncing around like a teenager. You're making me feel old.'

'You look old.' She tilted her head, sparkling green eyes inspecting him unabashedly. 'James, you've become conservative.'

'I've always been conservative,' he retorted, loosening the tie she clearly disapproved of. 'You just never looked at me properly before.'

She giggled. 'Oh, I looked,' she said lightly. 'All the girls looked at you, you silly man. Didn't you notice?'

'Not you,' he said dryly. He'd have noticed that. Tessa had only ever looked at one man. 'And, tell me, what have you done with poor Richard? Left him behind again to do the work while you tour the sights?'

Instantly Tessa paled, and James stiffened, wondering what he'd said wrong. 'Oh, God,' he said dully. 'You two, you haven't. . .?'

'We're separated,' she said huskily. 'I'm sorry. I thought you knew.'

Know? How could he know? He hadn't seen either of them in ages and Tessa hadn't mentioned a thing in her missives. 'Richard's. . .?'

'Working in The States. In Washington. Seattle, Washington, I mean, not DC. It's a good job, I think.'

'When?'

'Twelve months ago.' She smiled again, but he could see a slight wobbliness to it now. 'It's all right,' she insisted, but her pallor told him it wasn't. 'It was for the best,' she added, the throaty edge to her voice and the slim gold band she still wore on her left ring finger confirming his opinion that she didn't think it was at all. 'We'd had our ups and downs over the years. It was no one's fault.'

Those last words and the deliberate way she straightened her shoulders told him everything, and inwardly he swore, using the excuse of discarding his jacket to turn away from her lest she saw his anger. Richard was an ignorant, stupid bastard, he raged. Clearly the faults of his youth had not settled after marriage to Tessa.

Although how the hell he'd managed to find targets for his wandering hands while stuck in the middle of Sadakh during a civil war, James couldn't imagine. Then he remembered what had happened on Richard's stag night and felt sick.

'And I hear you've been canvassing my patients,' he said, collecting himself and turning back to her, his expression carefully neutral. 'Hope they made it worth your while.'

Her eyes brightened immediately. 'James, they were wonderful.' She beamed. 'I'm not going to bother doing the rounds with my begging bowl next time—I'm just going to sit in your waiting room. Delia Buttrose-Allen's written me a cheque for enough to order a new incubator and the sterilising equipment I've been begging for. And that's just the start.'

'Good.' Pleased to see her colour had returned to normal, he directed her through to his kitchen. 'It was a good day for you to come. Not all my patients are that affluent.'

'That's not what I hear.' She perched on a stool, watching him as he selected a wine and opened the bottle. 'Great car. Beautiful house. Prestigious teaching hospital job. Hugely successful private practice. You've really made it, James.'

James rolled his eyes, knowing what would come next. 'No, Tessa.'

CHAPTER TWO

BUT James's refusal did nothing to deflect Tessa. 'Don't you ever wonder if there isn't something more to life — ?'

'No.' He grinned at her, enjoying her predictability if not the argument. 'Forget it.'

'Six months,' she pleaded. 'All right, three,' she said urgently when he looked away to pour their drinks. 'Six weeks.'

'Don't I send you enough money?'

'You're my biggest contributor.' She took the glass of chilled white he offered her and accepted his toast wordlessly. 'But we've been trying to find a replacement surgeon for months now.'

'I know.' He sipped the cool liquid, enjoying its fragrant dryness. Although he hadn't realised that Richard hadn't been with her—he'd assumed she'd merely been looking for a second surgeon. 'You've written to me four times since Christmas.'

'Five times.' She was flushing now, and the colour highlighted the vivid green of her eyes. 'And the agency here's had no more luck. Jean-Paul's been with us for three years but he must leave in September, and he's been trying as hard as all of us, but we still haven't found anyone to take his place.'

And with Richard gone, she wouldn't have a surgeon at all. James wondered if his friend had made any effort to find a replacement for himself. His fists clenched. Knowing Richard, probably not.

'What about through the Red Cross? Can they suggest someone suitable?'

'They need every volunteer they can find themselves.' She ran a hand through her hair, leaving the short fringe spiky and ruffled, and he felt a sudden urge to smooth

17

it. 'As does every other organisation. The world isn't getting any more peaceful. But, James, if you could just see the children—'

'Tessa, I'd like to help.' He picked up his glass and held it to keep his hands occupied. 'You know I would. But my waiting list at the Free's almost eighteen months—there's even a six-month wait to get onto my outpatient list.'

'And there's your private list,' she added, mock-sympathetically. 'All those terribly urgent varicose veins...'

'I know.' He sighed. 'I know varicose veins probably don't seem the most important condition in the world to treat but people still suffer.'

'And I'm sure they pay wonderfully well,' Tessa teased. Then she smiled, a broad, generous smile that dazzled him. 'And I'm thrilled that you're doing so well, really. Particularly as so much of the money seems to make its way to my hospital. And you know I wouldn't ask if I wasn't desperate—'

'Rubbish.' He swung a stool round so he faced her across the breakfast bar. 'You've been trying to get me out there for years.'

She laughed. 'Well, that is true,' she conceded, 'but only because we need you so badly. And I think you'd be great there. You'd love Sadakh.'

'Trauma surgery on a shoestring budget in a tent in the desert in the middle of a civil war?' He grinned. 'Sounds like heaven.'

She poked out a small pink tongue. 'It's not a tent.'

He studied the pale curve of her mouth, wanting to provoke her tongue again. 'It was a tent.'

'It hasn't been for five years. We've got a proper hospital now. Don't you read anything I send you?'

'Occasionally.' He tore his gaze away from her mouth and saw how offended she was. 'Come on, Tessa. Be fair. Your letters are like novels. If I read every word I'd have no time for operating.'

'I like to keep you informed.'

'I like it that you keep me informed.' Suddenly restless, he finished his drink and refilled it, topping up hers as well although she'd only taken a few sips.

He walked to the refrigerator and pulled the door open, wondering what they could eat. He didn't want to take her out for dinner, he realised. He wanted her all to himself.

Then he stilled, not sure he liked that feeling. 'And I'm only joking,' he added, dragging his attention back to their conversation about her letters. 'I do read all of them.'

'Good.' She smiled. 'Thank you for persuading the hospital to send their used stuff.'

'Glad I could help.' He returned her smile. 'Was any of it useful?'

'Everything.' She took a delicate sip of the wine and he saw movement beneath the creamy skin of her throat as she swallowed. 'They sent loads. Catheters, syringes and needles, expired antibiotics that would otherwise be thrown out. It was like Christmas for us.'

'Good.' He frowned at the contents of his fridge. His housekeeper kept it stocked but tonight nothing looked particularly appetising. 'You still eat pizza?'

'Love it.' The eyes were sparkling again. 'Like you'd love the food in Sadakh.'

'Curried goat?' His mouth twisted. 'I doubt it.'

'It's very healthy,' she insisted gaily. 'And totally organic.'

'Nice.' He reached for the telephone. 'Any requests?'

'Hot and spicy pepperoni. With anchovies.' At his grimace her grin widened. 'And extra chillies.'

James ordered a ham and mushroom pizza for himself and for Tessa the revolting mixture she'd requested, repeating the order to the doubtful assistant when she queried it and adding the extra capers Tessa requested while he was on the phone.

'Twenty minutes,' he told her, once the conversation had finished. 'More wine?'

'Just a little.' She lifted her still half-filled glass to meet the bottle he held. 'Six years in Sadakh. I'm out of practice.'

'Is alcohol forbidden?'

'Tolerated for foreigners.' Something he couldn't read flickered across her expression but then it was gone. She said, 'Richard always had his Scotch but I never wanted to offend anyone.'

James's mouth had tightened at the mention of her husband and he immediately changed the subject, diverting her into a conversation about mutual friends and what had happened in their lives during Tessa's years abroad.

The pizzas arrived. Beautiful late-evening summer sun penetrated the kitchen so he didn't suggest they moved into the dining room. They ate instead at the breakfast bar, not bothering with plates and using their fingers instead of cutlery.

Tessa, he noted approvingly, ate with gusto, uncaring that the juice from her food quickly smeared her hands and mouth.

She laughed at his distaste for the violent flavours of her meal. 'Try it,' she insisted, holding a wedge to his mouth and trying to push it in. 'Just one bite. You'll love it.'

'Get away.' But he was laughing too as he fended her off. 'God! It stinks.'

'Anchovies.' She peeled one off and ate it with exaggerated relish. 'Yum yum.'

'You're revolting,' he teased, although in reality he was finding her totally desirable. She had a zest for life, he realised, that had grown rather than diminished with the years. He envied that.

'I haven't had pizza in years.' Having almost finished hers now, she eyed the remains of his assessingly. 'Are you going to eat that?'

'Take it.' He shoved the box across. 'Want me to order another one?'

'This'll do.' She tore the slice into strips and ate them one by one, curling them into her mouth so he caught delicious glimpses of the little pink tongue that had taunted him earlier. 'Got any ice cream?'

'Sorry.' James wished he had. Briefly the thought of coating her in it drifted into his mind and he stood up, turning away abruptly and rocking his stool back so the metal leg scraped against the tiles. 'Coffee?'

'Tea, please.' Tessa had tugged some paper towels free from their holder and was wiping her face and mouth, clearly unaware of the tension that had driven him away from her. 'No milk. Two sugars.' She pushed herself off her stool. 'I'll go and clean up. Is there a bathroom down here?'

'Not a proper one. Use the one upstairs.'

He waited until she'd skipped out of the room, then lowered his head, bracing his arms against the bench— furious with himself. Even if Tessa and Richard were separated it was obvious she regretted it, he told himself fiercely.

And his easy assurance that he could maintain the shield of friendship he'd learned to use with Tessa now seemed insufferably smug. In reality he'd had no excuse for not anticipating he'd react like this—God knew, he always had. Even, he reminded himself savagely, long after it had become obvious that she was falling in love with his friend.

And long after Tessa's joy at finding love had finally driven it home to him that he had no right to say or do anything that might interfere with that happiness.

Had he been in love with her?

He stared down at the hard black and grey layered hues of the granite bench top, his fist clenching against its curved edge. He hadn't let himself consider that before— pragmatic at heart, it hadn't been something he'd wanted to contemplate. And now, he reflected, looking back, even with the gift of hindsight he wasn't sure. He'd been drawn to her, had wanted her and at the time that had seemed overwhelming.

There'd been times since when he'd wanted other women, too, not many like that, but some. But inevitably with them satiation had dulled his desire. Only with Tessa had it persisted. But, of course, with Tessa he'd never had the chance to become sated.

James drew himself up sharply, refusing to allow himself to become distracted by the provocative images that thought evoked.

Nothing had changed, he told himself grimly. Nothing. Whatever Richard's faults, his wife clearly loved him still. And that made desiring Tessa as pointless and immoral as it had ever been.

When she returned he frowned at her, determined to keep his reactions to her more rational. 'Did you say two sugars?' he asked doubtfully.

'Make it three.' She grinned at his expression. 'Sorry,' she said brightly, looking anything but. 'Am I offending your sensibilities?'

'All of them.' He tipped the sweetener into her drink, returning her grin. 'Ever heard of diabetes?'

'See about two cases in a bad year,' she said cheerfully, taking the cup from him. She sipped, then made an appreciative noise. 'No, most of my patients these days have got fairly basic problems.'

'Missing arms and legs?'

He watched her eyes cloud and cursed himself for the question. 'Along with the usual complement of Third World diseases,' she said quietly. 'We've one of the highest infant mortality rates in the world, only no one's taken any notice of the statistics I've collected. Plus tuberculosis, measles, leishmaniasis—you know the sorts of things.'

'Any plans to come home?'

'No.' She tilted her head, regarding him serenely. 'There's too much to do.'

'How are you going to cope without a surgeon?'

'Terribly.' She took another hurried sip of her tea. 'I can do the basics, of course. Richard was a good teacher and I've had a lot of time to learn. Wound surgery, amputations, bowel resections, hernias—that sort of thing—but the more complicated stuff, the reconstructions and the organ repair work, is beyond me.' She smiled at his expression. 'Even a paediatrician can learn to operate, James. I've even passed my primary. Don't be so stuffy.'

'I'm not being stuffy,' he countered heavily. 'I'm over-awed. I didn't realise you had anything to do with the operative side of things.'

'Needs must,' she recited. 'In emergencies it's all hands on deck—there's no choice.' Then she tilted her head in that alert, bird-like way he was coming to recognise. 'Of course, with someone like you working with me. . .'

'Enough.' The word was gruff but his rebuttal was less adamant now than earlier. Perhaps he could arrange some leave, he thought, wondering. Wondering also at the madness of seeing more of her, considering his reaction to her tonight. But Tessa and her hospital's need for a surgeon made his doubts seem selfish, self-important. Leave wouldn't be easy to organise but possibly he could manage a few weeks. 'Tessa, I don't know. It'd take time to organise.'

She was holding herself very still. 'But. . .perhaps?'

'Perhaps.' He frowned, adding carefully, 'Give me some time.'

Tessa's eyes widened hopefully but instead of saying anything about that her gaze dropped abruptly to the floor behind him and she said, 'The kitten's awake.'

He blinked. 'What?'

'The kitten.' She pointed behind him. 'Look, she's playing with the cork.'

James turned and saw a tiny black cat playing with the wine cork which must have tumbled from the bench, batting it until it moved then leaping upon it. 'Tessa. . .?' It was almost a growl.

'She followed me,' she said quickly. 'All the way from the tube. I took her back. I knocked on all the doors but I couldn't find anyone who'd ever seen her before. The vet said she was too thin. She thought she'd probably been abandoned. But she's taken note of your address in case someone comes looking for her. I ordered all her shots this afternoon. She's fully immunised and I got you a litter box and some toys. Everything's in the laundry for the moment but since it's so warm you might want to move it outside—'

'This is insane.'

'James, look at those eyes.'

And he did. And they were huge and green and beautiful, and they reminded him of Tessa's.'

'She's so tiny.'

He looked at her despairingly. 'I haven't the time to look after her,' he said deeply. 'I'm hardly ever home.'

'Monica next door says she'll be happy to look after her when you're away, and she says your housekeeper loves cats—she always plays with hers when they come over. She's here every day, Monica told me, so there's someone else who'll help keep her company. And Monica's promised to make you up a special food mixture for her for the first few months. She makes it herself—loads of calcium—it sounds very nutritious. Her parents breed cats, you know, so she knows all about them.'

James sighed. In five years he'd barely spoken with his neighbour—didn't even know her name. Tessa had been here five minutes and they already sounded friends. 'Does she have a name?' he said, resigning himself.

'What do you think about "Sooty"?' she asked, smiling.

'Unoriginal.' He crouched to tickle the furry creature but the movement was too sudden and she arched up, fur spiking, and spat at him. ' "Prickles" is more apt,' he said softly, coaxing the kitten with a gentle finger behind her ears until she stepped forward and rubbed her nose into his palm.

'She likes you.'

'Hmm.' James wasn't convinced but it seemed that the decision had been made. 'I suppose I should be grateful it wasn't a Great Dane that followed you home.' And then he looked back at her and saw the way she was biting at her lower lip. 'I'll be expecting a bill from the vet, then?'

'Yes.' Tessa smiled at him, obviously relieved he understood. 'Thanks. I'm afraid I couldn't quite afford—'

'Forget it.' He tickled the creature once more and then rose, smiling as it pounced on one of his shoelaces. 'I think my income can stretch to looking after one kitten.'

'After this afternoon, I think it can, too,' she said easily, her momentary embarrassment obviously evaporated. Taking her tea, she eased herself from the stool and strolled away from him into the twilight gloom of his conservatory. 'Your practice rooms are sumptuous. It was like being in a luxury hotel. I even asked your secretary where the pool was.'

James laughed, suspecting that Lucy wouldn't have been amused. She tended to take everything to do with him and the practice very seriously. He collected his coffee and followed her. 'What did she say?'

'She wasn't impressed.' Tessa settled herself on one of the benches that lined the octagonal walls of the glass conservatory and tucked one slender leg under herself. She lifted her head and he saw her inhale the delicate rose scent that filtered through the louvres from the garden outside with obvious appreciation.

But her attention returned to him as he took the seat beside her, and she regarded him steadily over her mug. 'This is beautiful.'

'Yes.' He watched her. 'You shouldn't be bearing all the problems of the hospital yourself. Isn't there anybody who can help you?'

'It's my project,' she said calmly. 'I established everything. It's my job to keep it working.'

'What about the agency here in London?'

'Busy with a dozen other projects. And naturally we're not eligible for any aid assistance so our income is far less significant than their other enterprises.'

'And once this. . .Jean-Paul person leaves how many ex-pat staff will you have? Just the three others?'

'Two Dutch nurses and our Finnish anaesthetist,' she confirmed. She shifted her legs slightly, swivelling more to face him with one slender arm stretching along the back of the bench. 'Plus seven local workers we've trained ourselves.'

'And the war?'

'Times of fighting, times of peace. There's stability, more or less, in the capital now and perhaps that will spread, perhaps not. It hasn't yet. Control of the area we service is still divided between the region's warlords, each with his own army, and they still fight each other periodically.'

'Still seeing blast injuries from the land-mines?'

'The leader of the UN clearing operation was killed last month,' she said sadly. 'He was a Canadian—a very nice man. Several others were injured. There are still thousands of Russian mines around but without lasting peace I don't think there'll be any more attempts to clear them.'

It was dark now and there was no moon. He could barely see her face but he could feel her next to him, could smell the lovely, clean soap scent of her skin. 'It might never end,' he said quietly.

'I know that.' He felt her move slightly but couldn't tell in what way. 'But I'm pleased with the work I do,' she said softly.

'Don't you miss Britain?'

'Sometimes.' She sounded surprised by the question. 'Wimbledon.'

'And pizza?'

She laughed. 'Yes. Of course.'

He wanted to ask her if she missed the people—her family, friends, him. But he hesitated, sensing he might not like the answer.

Deciding that Tessa probably thought that the loss of contact with people here was a small price to pay for the satisfaction she got from her work, he stayed quiet.

Tessa had been a teenager, then a student and junior doctor during times of great upheaval in the world, where images of famine and war had dominated the headlines. Knowing how sensitive she was, he understood how she'd been touched by that, but for Tessa the emotion itself hadn't been enough. She'd wanted to help. Passionately. Practically.

And by the time they'd all met she'd been very sure of what she wanted to do with her life, determined to use her skills where they could be most useful. He hadn't been surprised to hear of her plans to work in the Third World.

The surprise at first in those early years had been that Richard had shared her vocation. Until he'd met Tessa Richard had never mentioned anything about aid work, and at the time James had privately wondered if Richard's motives had been less than altruistic.

There'd been more of a craving both for Tessa and unconventional adventure than true vocation, he'd suspected, behind Richard's enthusiasm in the beginning.

But that enthusiasm had been sustained, even after it was obvious Tessa had been sharing his bed. Later when Richard had offered to buy her a car Tessa had refused, preferring to stick with her bicycle and telling him that if he had that much spare cash he ought to be sending the funds to charity.

To Richard's credit—and James's astonishment—that was exactly what he'd done and that, together with Richard's enthusiasm for the work the pair were planning abroad, had forced James to accept that his friend had changed, making his own feelings for Richard's future wife seem disloyal and sordid.

She was in love with Richard, he'd told himself sharply and repeatedly. And it had seemed that Richard was right for her.

Until Richard's stag party.

Abruptly he turned cold. He jerked himself away from thinking about that now and turned his attention back to Tessa, noting broodingly her air of contentment as she relaxed against the bench—so at variance with his own dark memories. 'Does Sadakh feel like home to you now?'

'Yes.'

'More than Britain?'

He felt her hesitation. 'It's different,' she said slowly.

'Tell me.'

'I'll bore you.'

He allowed himself a small smile. 'No, you won't.' Tessa's letters, her enthusiasm and passion, had kindled a genuine interest in Sadakh in him over the years.

'Sadakh has a magic that I can never describe to anyone who hasn't been there,' she said softly. 'It's vast and barren and the air is so clear that it cuts you when you breathe and the mountains are sharp, like massive blades above you wherever you move.'

She laughed, a little self-consciously, he thought, but her voice was eager. 'In England you forget about the earth,' she continued. 'The earth as a planet, I mean. But in Sadakh you think about that constantly. If you stare hard enough at the horizon it feels as if you'll see right off the edge of the earth and into space. And the skies are amazing—blazing, terrible blues. It's. . .it's ancient,' she said finally. 'It moves me.'

Her descriptions had made him almost breathless. 'And the people?'

'Gentle, patient, mysterious, and at the same time fierce and vengeful and earthy.' She laughed again, softly this time. 'Am I making sense?'

'No.' He smiled as her laughter deepened, capturing the hand she lifted to shove against his shoulder and holding it fractionally before releasing it back to her.

'Come and see a sunrise,' she urged. 'You'll be hooked.'

'Hung, more like,' he murmured. 'I can see my patients stringing me up and letting me drop if I tell them I'm leaving. And God knows what my juniors would do— they've worked hard to get on to my rotation.'

'They'd cope.' She sounded confident. 'They'd understand you were going on to better things.'

'No, they wouldn't. All they'd know is that I was leaving.' He went and turned on the light, deciding that the intimacy of the dark room was not conducive to sensible discussion.

When he came back to her she blinked up at him. 'Is it healthy to encourage that sort of dependence?'

He hesitated, realising he must have sounded smug and self-centred where he'd only wanted to explain why it would be so difficult to leave. 'I know I'm not indispensable,' he said deeply. 'Any surgeon could do my job.'

'Technically, if not with the same panache,' she teased, her mouth twitching. 'For the first time in years I think you're definitely wavering, James Hyatt.'

'You obviously need help,' he admitted heavily.

'Yes.' She smiled. 'I hoped all my poetic words wouldn't be wasted.'

'They'd never be that.' And her descriptions had touched him, moved him more, probably, than logic ever could have. He took his seat again, moving back a little so there was more space between them. 'But you might find another surgeon before Jean-Paul leaves.'

'I might.' But she didn't sound confident.

'Do you need money for more advertising?' he asked, deliberately making his tone businesslike.

'Of course.' She touched his arm lightly with her hand. 'James, you already give a great deal.'

'I'll do an extra set of varicose veins a month,' he said dryly. 'Does that make you feel better?'

'Infinitely.' Her eyes had started to sparkle again. 'You know how to ease my conscience.'

'Since when have you had a conscience when it comes to asking for money?'

'Not since Sadakh,' she admitted unapologetically. 'Sorry.'

James laughed. They talked, for what seemed like a brief time, laughed and argued gently.

And then she stood up and yawned and stretched her long, slender arms, looked outside and said, 'Oh, heavens! I'm supposed to be at Heathrow by seven.'

James started. He met her appalled look uncomprehendingly, checked his watch and then lifted the kitten gently from his lap onto a cushion and stood too, startled. It was almost six-thirty. Outside it had become light hours ago yet until that second he'd not given the time a thought. They'd talked all night. 'I'll drive you. It shouldn't take too long at this hour.'

'I meant to catch the tube,' she said urgently, pushing her small feet into the sandals she'd discarded earlier, 'but a lift will be great. Thanks. I can't believe I didn't even notice. . .'

She looked up at him, her eyes luminescent. 'I'm sorry I kept you awake,' she said huskily. 'You should have told me to shut up.'

She was soft and still and suddenly vulnerable and James looked at her and almost reached for her but the kitten made a tiny noise and Tessa looked at her and it was too late.

'What time's your flight?' he asked, suddenly brisk, and they were rushing, hurrying, bumping each other in their haste to get upstairs to one of his spare rooms where she'd piled her things.

'Just before eight, I think. There's still time.'

She lifted a large knapsack, preparing to slide her arms

into the straps but he took it from her and carried it himself.

'To Paris first,' she said, thanking him with a quick smile as she collected a battered holdall and slung it crosswise across her chest along with an embroidery and leather handbag. 'Then I connect.'

James took the last bag, a plastic sack that appeared to be full of newspapers, and followed her downstairs. 'Passport? Ticket?'

'No.' At the front door she turned around, flushing, and raced past him towards the kitchen, returning seconds later with a small canvas-like holder which she slung around her neck then stuffed carelessly inside her shirt.

Within twenty minutes they'd cleared the already congested streets around his home and were on the A4, soaring over Hammersmith—making the most of the relative calm of the west-heading lane, compared to the opposite one which was only just moving.

Tessa, he noticed with amusement, despite her earlier panic, was enjoying the ride. She experimented with the CD system, then the controls that adjusted the windows and finally she stretched out her legs and wiggled them appreciatively.

'There is something to be said for luxury,' she said contentedly.

He smiled. 'You don't drive one of these in Sadakh?'

'All the time.' The eyes were sparkling again. 'No, the hospital has an ancient Jeep that's kept running by magic.' She grinned. 'I think I'm starting to understand why you're not immediately agreeing to tear yourself away from this cold place. I could get used to the car.'

He changed lanes and accelerated onto the motorway. 'Want me to buy you one?'

'No.' He glanced at her quickly and saw that she was as startled as he was by the offer. 'Do you mean that?'

'I hope not,' he joked, but he wasn't sure. He wanted to give her something, he realised. Not just towards the hospital, but something that would make her happy. But a car? That was ridiculous, wasn't it? And wouldn't she just tell him to give the money to charity instead? 'Would you use one?'

'No. It's too much.'

'That doesn't sound like you.'

'I can hardly believe it myself,' she confessed. 'Quickly, put it in writing before I take it back.'

'Would you use it?' he asked again.

'Women aren't allowed to drive in Sadakh.'

He pulled out smoothly and overtook two lorries, then pulled back into the left lane, ready for the approaching Heathrow turn-off. 'What about when you come to London?'

'No.' She sounded bemused. 'That would be silly. I'm hardly ever here.'

'OK. Bad idea.' Suddenly tense, he took the bends then dared a brief glance, but her wrinkled nose and the tiny, earnest lines between her brows told him that he'd merely puzzled her.

'James, I'll understand if you can't come,' she said slowly a few minutes later. 'You shouldn't feel guilty. You do more than anyone, as it is.'

He realised that she thought guilt was behind his offer of the car. As it probably was, he told himself, electing not to examine his motives any further.

She swivelled towards him slightly. 'I know that I've put a lot of pressure on you and I know that isn't fair but I just feel so helpless at the moment. You're the only surgeon I know who's even interested—' She stopped. 'I understand how busy you are and the hospital's not your responsibility,' she finished gently.

But she hesitated and laughed, a light, tinkling laugh that made him smile, too. 'Oh, heavens. I might wish I hadn't said that.'

'Too late.' He slowed. 'Which terminal?'

'Four.'

As soon as he'd parked she scrambled out. 'I should be in time,' she said, returning seconds later with a trolley.

'James, I can manage. You must have to get to work.'

She was right. He didn't have time to wait. But he wanted to. He loaded the bags onto the trolley. 'When do you think you'll be back?'

'I don't know.' She looked preoccupied now, her mind obviously on the journey ahead. 'I might be able to come in a few months for some more fund-raising, but it might be as much as a year or longer. I can't be sure.'

'Let me know.' He hesitated. 'And let me know in a month if you still haven't found someone else. OK?'

'Yes.' Her voice was husky.

'I can't promise.'

'I know.' But she smiled. 'Thanks, James. You're wonderful.'

'I don't know, Tessa.' He leaned forward, intending—*determined*—to kiss her cheek, but instead he touched her mouth in a brief, hard kiss that did nothing to assuage his frustration but, judging from her sudden pallor, went a long way towards startling Tessa.

Wordlessly, he slammed the boot closed and returned to his seat, raising one hand briefly in farewell as he drove away—fast.

CHAPTER THREE

TESSA crouched over Mustaf's swollen leg. He'd been blasted by a land-mine four months earlier during a clearing operation. Jean-Paul had had to amputate his leg from a few inches below his knee, but the stump had become infected, delaying healing and later infecting the bone.

He'd now been on the best antibiotics she had for four weeks, but the remains of his lower leg had become tender and the high temperatures he'd been spiking suggested that the infection was failing to resolve.

Osteomyelitis, or infection in the bone, was a rare complication in the hospital. Given the conditions in Sadakh and the risk of sepsis from war injuries, they always paid strict attention to cleaning wounds to diminish the risk of infection.

But Mustaf was poor, and his nutritional status had reflected that, making him more susceptible to complications than a patient living in Britain would have been.

In the local dialect she asked him about the pain, nodding when he described the deep aching which had been keeping him awake. He told her that the fever had racked him with shivers the night before.

His dark, searching eyes probed hers calmly. 'Perhaps it is not meant to get better,' he said, with the sort of fatalistic resignation Tessa had grown to expect from his people. 'Perhaps it is my time.'

Despite his calm, she decided that his wife and two children and the rest of his extended family would feel less resigned. 'There will be an aeroplane soon,' she explained, not being more specific about the time because, although she expected it later that day, such things were unpredictable in Sadakh. 'A new surgeon will come. I want to wait for his advice.'

'Of course.' He seemed neither surprised nor excited. 'I also wait.'

Tessa moved to the next bed, formally greeting her patient's relatives as she waited for them to clear the bed. Outside of a basic and unappetising gruel, the hospital didn't supply food for patients who had family locally and consequently the wards were often crowded with relatives, visiting and preparing food.

'Better today?' she asked, using English this time. Hafeez had been a member of the same UN-affiliated mine-clearing operation as Mustaf and he'd learned the basics of the language from the team's Canadian supervisor.

The programme had been abandoned four months previously after the death of the supervisor, and Hafeez's injuries had come from a recent mortar attack on his village.

Although far from fluent in English, he was proud of his skills and enjoyed showing off his abilities to his relatives. His command of the language increased his status enormously within his family.

'Yes, it is so. I am better.' His smile was gentle as he took a few experimental deep breaths for her. It had been two weeks since shrapnel from a shell had pierced his chest, puncturing his right lung. Jean-Paul had operated and the day before Tessa had removed the final chest drain.

She tapped out his chest, concentrating on the area where the blood and air had collected previously. The note was resonant, suggesting only inflated lung beneath her fingers.

Then she pressed the bell of her stethoscope across his back, years of practice enabling her to be skilled at editing out the background noise of the busy ward. His breath sounds were full and symmetrical and she tugged the tubes out of her ears and straightened, smiling. 'Very good,' she said lightly. 'Very, very good. Are you happy to leave tomorrow?'

His face lifted. 'Tomorrow? I am very pleased.'

'Back in five days for the stitches,' she added, mimicking removing the thread to increase the chance of him understanding but making a mental note to return later when he was alone so she could speak to him in his own language.

Hafeez was the last adult patient she needed to see so after him she went to the children's ward. Here she felt at home. Six years in Sadakh had given her a broad-based general training, but her speciality in Britain had been paediatrics and children's medicine was her first love.

The children's ward was almost always noisy, and the din that greeted her today was not unusual. Her patients themselves were generally quiet, but there was constant bustle and wailings from their siblings and relatives.

Rabdul, a seven-year-old boy with cheeky brown eyes, came racing up to her, moving with youthful adroitness on the crutch which had come to replace the leg he'd lost in a rocket attack on his village, the rival village to the one Hafeez came from. 'Today, today?' he chanted. 'Today is today?'

'Yes.' She smiled into his beaming face and crouched, inspecting the stump of his amputated leg. Well healed and healthy, there was no longer the slightest need for him to stay. 'I can't believe you're so eager to leave me,' she teased, switching to his language. 'Are we so horrible?'

'Horrible, no.' He was still grinning. 'But I am fast now. I want to show my village.'

'You're very fast.' She knew how hard he'd worked to get mobile again. 'OK. You can leave.'

He did a fast pirouette of joy, then called to his mother who came to Tessa with two of her seven other children. The small woman clutched at her hand tearfully, thanking her for her help, and Tessa squeezed the dry, calloused hand gently.

They were the same age, she and Rabdul's mother, but the other woman's face was worn and creased with the strain of poverty and the work of raising her children.

And Tessa reflected that by Sadakhi standards she was almost middle-aged. Life expectancy for women here was forty-six, for men only a year more. And her husband, along with much of her husband's family, had been killed in the same attack that had injured Rabdul.

Tessa had deliberately kept Rabdul in hospital, along with one of his sisters who'd only suffered minor injuries, as one way of trying to ease the burden on their mother while she and the surviving villagers rebuilt their homes and their lives.

Now, though, it was time the children went home. And, judging from their mother's joy, she was ready for them.

Rabdul and his sister had already collected their belongings together, and through the little blanket that enclosed their things Tessa could see the shape of the Paddington Bears she'd brought them each from London.

It had been a sentimental gesture. And at seven and six, she'd wondered if they'd be a little wary of the childishness of the gifts. Children in Sadakh grew up fast—they played with ammunition, not toys, and in a few years Rabdul would be old enough for his first Kalashnikov. To her delight, though, they'd loved the bears.

She shook Rabdul's hand and waved as the little group left, Rabdul skipping ahead on his crutch. Leaning against the doorframe and watching them go, she started slightly when Helena, one of their nurses, touched her shoulder.

'All right?'

'A little fragile,' she conceded. 'There's been more tension between the villages.' Each village, Rabdul's and Hafeez's, was loyal to rival warlords, and the attacks had been a symptom of that rivalry. 'There might be more trouble.'

'What do you think will happen?'

'I'll discharge Hafeez tomorrow if his lung stays inflated.' Tessa knew that he had some influence within the village. 'He's respected there. He'll talk sense—he might be able to talk them out of retribution.'

The Dutch woman nodded. 'How many have they lost these past months? Ten?'

'Nine in Rabdul's village.' Tessa frowned. 'Nine dead, twenty injured. Three dead in Hafeez's village, but that included one of the militia chief's cousins so there is still fury about that.' These attacks had been the first major incidents in the region in almost a year but there'd been several skirmishes since, and she worried that the conflict between the various factions was beginning to escalate again.

The country had been embroiled in wars for decades— conflict with the Russians had merely been the biggest one. And while that war had temporarily brought the factions together, united against a common enemy, after the retreat the tribal and political divisions had become obvious again, with the outbreak of fresh civil strife.

But dwelling on it and brooding changed nothing and she'd been here too long not to have acquired at least some sense of fatalism about the troubles. Making a determined effort to brighten herself up, she caught the sound of a small plane far above. She looked up, stiffening.

'That must be it.' Helena looked suddenly as excited as she felt. 'I've been listening all morning.'

'Me, too.' Tessa could still hardly believe he was coming. Even a month, she'd told him when it became obvious she'd find no replacement for Jean-Paul, would help. But until she actually saw him she knew it wouldn't sink in that he was really here.

Mohammed, one of their locally trained paramedics, had obviously heard the noise, too, because he was strolling towards the Jeep.

Tessa passed Helena the notes she'd been carrying. 'I'll go with him.'

Mohammed grinned laconically as she dashed towards him. 'No hurry,' he said easily. 'Plenty of time.'

'I want to be there when it lands,' she panted, leaping into the grumbling vehicle. She wanted to see his face. She wanted to read his first impressions of this beautiful country. 'Pity it's not sunset.'

'Lucky it isn't,' Mohammed said sensibly, drawing slowly out onto the scarred dirt track that served as a road. 'The tracer fire might frighten this excellent doctor.'

Tessa glanced towards the hills but they'd been silent for the last few days, and the pilots that came here were skilled at avoiding the fire. They hadn't ever lost a plane, not even at the height of the war.

'My excellent doctor won't scare easily,' she said lightly, smiling a little and wondering. In London James had seemed powerfully at ease with his place in the world, and she was looking forward to seeing how he dealt with life in Sadakh. 'But don't let anybody shoot at him.'

'I promise.' But Mohammed was grinning.

'I'll be watching you,' she warned, giving him her sternest expression. When Richard and she had first come out the local men, including Mohammed, had enjoyed taking the odd pot-shot at the ground beside Richard's feet. They'd laughed at the way he'd danced. For them there was a macho pride in showing no reaction to such provocation, but Richard had never quite mastered staying cool.

But Mohammed's grin didn't falter. 'There it is,' he said, pointing to the small speck ahead of them as it began its steep, spiralling descent. 'Here comes your excellent doctor.'

A couple of minutes later the tiny plane taxied towards them. Tessa had given the airstrip guards gifts of cigarettes and American dollars to minimise any difficulties, and they didn't even look up from their posts as Mohammed drove gently forward to collect the cargo.

As she swung herself out of the Jeep James, climbing out on to the wing of the small plane, paused. He looked up at the mountains that soared against the eastern sky, his expression solemn.

She gave him a few moments to gather his impressions but, despite her determination to give him time, couldn't stay quiet any longer. 'James!'

His gaze dropped and he grinned as she ran towards him, leaping to the ground to catch her and swinging her around as she remembered he had in London.

'I can't believe you're here,' she cried, hugged against his chest.

'Neither can I,' he said dryly, releasing her and nodding towards the plane. 'I said a prayer or two as we were coming down.'

'It's always like that.' Tucking her hand into the crook of his elbow and laughing and skipping in her excitement, she led him towards where the pilot and Mohammed had begun to unload the plane. Turnaround time here had to be short—any more than fifteen minutes and the guards became restless. 'They come in steep to avoid the rockets.'

At his sharp look she laughed again, releasing him. 'There weren't any today,' she reassured him. 'Relax. It's peaceful right now.'

'Good. Very good.' Giving her a doubtful look, he stepped forward and helped Mohammed with a crate that looked heavy—nodding to the smaller man as Tessa performed quick introductions.

With the four of them working, it took only a short time to unload the small plane's cargo, and ten minutes later the plane took off.

Tessa insisted that James sat in the front of the Jeep and she perched on a box in the open-topped back for the short journey back to the hospital. 'I need your advice on so much,' she said eagerly, her voice uneven as the Jeep jolted over the rough ground. 'I've someone with osteomyelitis, I've a child with a cleft palate who's ready for surgery and—'

'And you've hurt yourself.' Drawing his brows

together, he took the hand she'd been bracing herself
with. He studied the faintly puckered scar and stroked it
lightly. 'What did you do?'

'Just a burn.' Tessa snatched her hand back and tucked
it behind her back, smiling to allay his suspicions—not
wanting him to see that it had started to tremble.

Tall and darkly handsome, James had always been
striking, and the years had made him more so. Today,
casually dressed in worn jeans and an open-necked, faded
blue cotton shirt, he made her toes curl.

Altogether too appealing for comfort, she noted breathlessly, even more determined after seeing him again to
overcome the attraction that prickled her skin.

Her shaken response to his chaste farewell kiss
at Heathrow had been embarrassingly teenage-like.
Heavens, she'd been married for years, she'd told herself.
And James was a friend. A good friend, but nothing else.
Yet with that faint, probably unconscious, touch of his
mouth, he'd made her feel like she imagined one of her
young nieces might on meeting a favourite pop star.

But, despite the frissons of anxiety that stemmed from
remembering that and now from feeling herself react so
strongly to his casual touch, her hospital needed his skills
and she was thrilled he was here. 'I've also got a child,
I think, with TB—confined to her fingers. I've never
seen a case before.'

'What did you burn it on?'

'The steriliser.' She and Mohammed exchanged quick
grins. He'd been there when she'd done it, and in his
concern he'd shouted at her as if she were one of his
children, cursing her impatience and carelessness.

She hadn't minded but later he'd been embarrassed
about his outburst and she still enjoyed teasing him about
it. 'And don't bother telling me off,' she added, to James.
'Mohammed's already done it.'

'Always hurrying.' Mohammed swerved gently to
avoid a pot-hole, then looked back at her, his dark eyes
twinkling. 'Tell me, what is the rush in life?'

'The rush is trying not to miss lunch,' she said, rolling her eyes. 'Mohammed, I can walk faster than this.'

'Suits me fine.' James tipped his head back, lifting his face to the mountains and to the sun. 'After that flight I'd be happy with snail-slow.'

She put her hand through the bar and ruffled his hair, enjoying its clean dark warmth. 'Poor James,' she said lightly. 'Were you frightened?'

'Petrified.' His eyes opened, gleamed blue-grey thoughtfulness into hers. 'Thanks for warning me.'

'It never even occurred to me.' She smiled. It was true. She'd spoken to him only twice and each time only briefly since she'd left London. In their last conversation he'd told her he was coming and she'd been so excited and there'd been so much to tell him that the journey itself hadn't entered her head. 'But you coped.'

'Barely.' But he seemed relaxed enough now.

'How's Prickles?'

'Thriving. She sends her love.'

Tessa smiled. 'Who's looking after her?'

'Jill, my housekeeper, and Monica next door, and another woman who lives near the corner and whom I'd never met before but apparently you have. They're all taking turns.'

'Janice.' Tessa nodded, remembering the woman she'd met when she was searching for the kitten's owner. 'Oh, I'm glad she introduced herself to you. She's a potter, you know. She showed me some of her work. It was beautiful.'

'Hmm.' James sounded less than convinced. 'I asked her to make me a milk jug for my mother's birthday. I thought something small and elegant but she made me a little fat cow.'

Tessa laughed. 'How did your mother like it?'

'She was polite.' His mouth twitched, but he didn't say anything more about it. Instead, he went on, 'I see what you meant that night, Tessa. The mountains are glorious.'

'Yes.' She smiled her pleasure at his reaction.

'And the sky. . .'

'I know.'

Mohammed looked amused. 'I think you are going to be the same as Tessa, James. The sky, the mountains. Always she is making me look up at her precious mountains. Always I am wondering what is so special. They are normal.'

'Not in London.' James hadn't taken his eyes off them. 'How far to the hospital?'

'Another mile or so.' Tessa looked pointedly at Mohammed. 'With anyone else driving, we'd be there by now.'

'Or stranded in a pot-hole,' said Mohammed, carefully driving around another crater. 'I remember one day, Richard—'

'Yes. Thank you.' Tessa stopped that anecdote before it could properly start, ignoring James's interested expression. 'James is a friend of Richard's,' she said meaningfully, reminding herself to tell the rest of the staff that. She didn't want James subjected to stories of her husband's antics.

'Acquaintance, more than friend, really,' said James unhelpfully, watching her. 'I haven't seen Richard in years. Got stuck in a pot-hole, did he?'

Tessa kicked the back of Mohammed's seat to try and stop him laughing. 'More than once,' she said tightly. 'Richard's always been something of a speed freak.'

She pointed ahead to the hospital complex. On the rim of a vast, scrubby desert plain, with foothills then mountains to the east, they'd built the three buildings which made up the complex a short distance from the edge of the town to try and make it a less likely target in an attack.

'The long block houses the wards and theatres,' she explained. 'Along with triage. The smaller one's Outpatients, and the one at the back is staff accommodation and the mess and kitchen and things.'

James straightened in his seat. 'It's bigger than I expected.'

'We started with just the ward block,' she explained. 'Well, actually, we started with big tents, but the ward block was built at the end of our first year here. Everything else has come gradually.'

Mohammed drove around behind the ward block and stopped outside the mess. They unpacked the things from the plane into the mess to be sorted later.

'Your precious newspapers,' James said, indicating a large plastic bag. 'Plus a few magazines I picked up.'

'Wonderful.' She beamed her appreciation—newspapers were the thing she missed second most from England, especially the weekend editions she'd requested. 'Peanut butter?'

'Crunchy.' He indicated another bag. 'All ten jars of the awful stuff. Relax. I didn't forget anything.'

A short while later, making tea for him in the mess, she frowned. 'Oh.' She'd been thoughtless. She'd been chattering about her patients, about cases she needed advice with and about problems they'd been having with equipment, forgetting that he'd had a long journey. 'Do you need to rest? We can leave work stuff until tomorrow, if you want. Things aren't too hectic here at present.'

Although they might be soon. Her eyes strayed briefly to the west, the direction of Mustaf's village. Less than five miles across the desert, they'd hear any fighting from here easily.

'I'm fine.' James was sprawled in a chair and he crossed one lean leg over the other with an easy grace, his narrowed blue-grey gaze regarding her with knowing warmth. 'Carry on, Tessa chatterbox. You know you'll burst if you don't tell me everything.'

That was exactly what she felt like—exactly. 'I still can't believe you're here,' she confessed. The water was bubbling and she turned off the gas and filled the teapot with the water, swilling it around. 'It's like a miracle. When we met in London you seemed to think you might manage it, but I didn't let myself hope too much.'

'The hospital wasn't happy at first,' he admitted, 'but they owed me the time. They've appointed an excellent locum, who was keen to cover my private work as well, so everything worked out easier than I expected. And, of course, I wanted to help.'

'Thank you.' She poured his drink and passed it to him, returning to stand against the bench to drink hers. 'We need you.'

He sipped his tea and promptly recoiled, making her laugh. 'You'll get used to it,' she said easily. She leaned forward, passing him the sugar after taking several generous spoonfuls herself. 'It grows on you.'

'I bet it grows on something.' He added a teaspoon of sugar to the opaque brew. 'Tastes like mould.'

'It's very healthy.' She looked up and smiled a greeting to the two nurses who'd come in—eyes wide, faces eager—obviously keen to meet their new surgeon. 'Helena, Monique—this is James Hyatt. James, the best two scrub and anaesthetic and everything nurses in the world—Helena DeBeer and Monique Visser.'

They shook hands and exchanged greetings and Tessa passed the other women tea.

Monique, the younger of the two nurses by almost a decade, was glowing. Her eyes widened as she inspected James with what looked like breathless relish. 'We are very delighted to have you,' she said excitedly, her pretty face pink and more lively than Tessa had seen it in months. She took the seat at the table beside him, shifting her chair a little closer towards him. 'Jean-Paul has only left a week ago but already we're needing a surgeon again. But you're not permanent, are you? How long are you staying?'

James and Tessa exchanged glances and he said, 'Three months, I think. Tessa's still trying to find someone who can stay long term.'

'James has a busy practice in London,' she said quickly. She hadn't given the others a time-frame, not

sure how long he'd want to commit himself for. Three
months was better than she'd hoped—he'd initially
thought six weeks might be the longest period of leave
he could get.

Monique barely acknowledged Tessa's words, her
gaze pinned on James. 'Have you worked somewhere
like this before?'

'No. I've only worked in London.'

'I'm Dutch but I've also worked in London,' she said
eagerly. 'Where have you worked there?'

James didn't seem especially surprised by Monique's
manner and Tessa realised he was probably accustomed
to attracting this sort of rapt attention from the women
he met. 'At the London and some time at the National,' he
said smoothly. 'Lately at the Free.' He swivelled slightly.
'Are you also from the Netherlands, Helena?'

'Yes.' Helena was much more relaxed than her colleague and she spooned sugar into her tea, glancing at
him casually as she passed the bowl back. 'I've been
here now for about four years.'

'And for me almost eighteen months.' Monique
touched his arm and squeezed it assessingly, her smile
widening in apparent approval of what she'd felt. She
asked James another question about London.

Tessa's eyebrows lifted. She looked at Helena but the
nurse shrugged, obviously less surprised than Tessa by
Monique's behaviour.

A skilled nurse, Monique was nevertheless young and
impressionable and at times Tessa worried that this
appointment was too demanding for her. She was less
self-contained than the rest of them. She needed more
attention and support but, even so, she'd proved herself
very good at her job.

Now, though, watching her almost childlike excitement at having a new person to talk with, Tessa began
to wonder if she needed some time back in Europe.

'If you enjoy it here,' she was saying to James, her

big brown eyes wide and appealing, 'perhaps you'll stay longer.'

'Perhaps.'

James looked at Tessa and she read his amusement and smiled at him, pleased—despite the confusion of her own feelings about him—that he hadn't found the younger woman's approach especially irresistible.

Then, cross with herself for, above all, she wanted him to stay and perhaps a relationship with Monique might achieve that, she gulped her tea and stood. 'I want to check the children,' she announced. 'Before lunch.'

When James made a move to stand, too, she held out her hand. 'No, James, stay. Stay here. Finish your tea. Monique will tell you a little about how we operate and I'll give you a tour after we've eaten.' Then she nodded at Helena. 'Ready to finish the round?'

'Sure.' Helena followed her out. 'You and your match-making,' she said, disapprovingly on their way across to the wards. 'You know he wanted to come with you.'

'I don't know why.' Tessa didn't look at her. 'He must be tired from the journey.'

Helena said, 'He didn't look especially so,' and Tessa acknowledged that that was true. The flights and connections from London took fifteen to eighteen hours but the hours had done nothing to blunt the vibrancy of his appeal.

Helena's blue gaze was shrewd. 'It won't work,' she said flatly. 'Axel and I were at least suited. James has nothing in common with Monique.'

Tessa speeded up. 'She's lively, young and very pretty. Why not? You've got Axel. I'm married. Monique's all alone.'

'You are not exactly married,' said Helena dryly.

'Richard's still my husband.' Tessa bounced ahead of her into the ward. 'And I'm sure Monique can look after herself.'

'More than you realise,' Helena muttered.

Tessa frowned. 'What?'

'Nothing.' Helena bent over a temperature chart. 'Damn! Ahmad is feverish again.'

'We'd better check him over.' Tessa looked around. She spotted the small boy outside among the chickens and she skipped outside and collected him. 'You little rascal,' she cried, lifting the giggling toddler into her arms. 'How did you get out here?'

She plonked him onto his bed and held him down while she gently tugged away the bandage that covered his abdomen, soothing him in his own language. 'Looks all right,' she said, checking his scar and probing the soft flesh around it. 'Urine?'

'Clear.'

Tessa listened to his chest, which was clear, checked his tonsils and ears and neck, then stared at the laughing child, puzzled. He'd recovered from his operation for a twisted bowel and he looked healthy, delightfully so. The only reason he was still in hospital was the mild fevers he kept spiking.

'Oh, for a decent lab,' she said feelingly. The only laboratory facilities she had access to had given her simple blood results, basic microbiology results—which had so far been negative—and a cross-match for when they needed to give a blood transfusion. A simple, non-specific test for infection that she could do had been negative, too.

'I'll see if I can find his mother.' Helena tucked the chart back under the mattress. 'She was here before and she might be hidden somewhere, feeding the baby.'

Tessa nodded. She looked up and saw James coming their way. His long and powerful legs crossed the gap in seconds.

'Any problems?' he asked quietly.

'Two-year-old boy, eleven days post-surgery,' she said, explaining the diagnosis. 'He's well, apart from these fevers that we can't account for. I thought you were finishing your tea?'

'I decided I'd rather be working,' he said dryly, his

shrewd eyes briefly meeting her deliberately innocent gaze. 'Thought about a collection of infection inside the abdomen?'

'Possibility, but he's very well. And the fever's not classically swinging.' She showed him the chart.

He examined it, then sat on the bed. She watched him gently palpate Ahmad's abdomen while the child stared up at him silently with wide eyes, obviously fascinated.

James said, 'Abdomen's soft. Spleen normal. Rectum?'

'Normal.'

He leaned forward and his knuckles brushed her thigh briefly as he tugged the stethoscope out of the pocket of her shirt.

The touch had been very casual, accidental even, and they'd touched before, but this time she froze. Their gazes collided, then locked and held for a few breathless, thoughtful seconds until James looked away and fitted the tubes into his ears.

Tessa's pulse was going 'thud thud thud' in her ears and she was calling herself so many names inside her head that she didn't even hear what he said next, and she blinked at him. 'What?'

'Normal bowel sounds,' he said quietly. He was watching her and she realised he'd seen exactly how much he'd flustered her. 'White count?'

'Normal. And sedimentation rate is normal.' Measuring the rate at which the blood cells separated from serum gave another broad indication of infection, but in this case it hadn't helped. 'That's about the limit of our haematology here.'

'Checked for viruses?'

She shook her head stiffly. 'Sorry, can't do.' Her voice sounded husky, bruised almost. 'All we can do is mix serum with a drop of formaldehyde—the mixture turns milky and solid in a number of infections, but Ahmad's didn't. It's another non-specific test but it's the best we can do.'

James seemed amused by her faintly defensive tone. 'CT scan?'

'Ha ha.' She looked down at their enthralled little patient, realising that James was merely playing with her. 'What do you think?'

'I wouldn't operate without better grounds.'

She nodded, agreeing with him. 'You're my mystery child,' she told Ahmad, making up her mind. His temperature spikes were not high enough to cause problems on their own and he wasn't in danger of having a seizure because of them.

'He can go home,' she told Helena as she returned alone. 'He's too well to keep here. When his family return we'll explain again about cooling him, and if he gets unwell they'll have to bring him back in.'

'They live in town,' she explained as she took James to see her next patient. 'Not far away. And I'll go and visit them in a few days.'

Another surgical patient among the children was a nine-month-old who'd presented with a twisted and stuck inguinal hernia the day after Jean-Paul had flown out. Hernia repairs, although involving complicated anatomy, were relatively straightforward in adults and she'd performed dozens in the past.

In babies, though, and especially when the tissues were as swollen as these had been it was like operating on tissue paper, and the surgery had been vastly more complex. But she'd had to operate or the child would have died. Today he was ready to be discharged.

James inspected the neat scar admiringly. 'You've missed your vocation,' he said quietly. 'This wouldn't have been easy. You should have been a surgeon.'

Absurdly pleased by his praise, she found herself flushing. 'Axel, our anaesthetist, helped,' she explained. 'He's seen hundreds before.'

After she'd finished with the children she took him to see Mustaf, needing his advice about the infection in his leg. James examined him, then went with her to inspect the rudimentary X-rays which were the best they could produce.

He confirmed her opinion that amputating Mustaf's femur just above the knee would be the best solution. 'In Britain we'd probably be able to avoid amputation,' he admitted, tapping the film of Mustaf's knee joint which, although swollen with fluid, didn't seem to have any bone damage. 'But here there's no realistic alternative.'

'I'll schedule it for the day after tomorrow,' she said, nodding. 'We've space to do it then.'

'Do you have a suitable prosthesis?'

'We'll be able to organise something. We brought some from London in the early days and Richard trained some of the local craftsmen to build and customise them.'

His head came up sharply at that and, wondering if he would be critical of them using semi-skilled staff, she said quickly, 'Obviously, they're not as perfect as you'd expect in the UK. But the craftsmen are true artists here and what they can build out of old tyres and wood and leather is amazing. Richard was a good teacher and they've had lots of experience so they're pretty good.'

'I'd like to see them working.' James tilted his head interestedly and she realised she'd misjudged him. 'You told me Richard was in Washington,' he said quietly. 'What's he doing there? Orthopaedics?'

'Trauma.' Her husband had trained in general surgery and had then switched to specialise in orthopaedics, his interest in the latter having always been the strongest. 'He's teaching as well. I think he's enjoying himself.'

'You keep in touch?'

'Of course.' She realised she was playing with her ring and, seeing James's gaze drop to it, she flushed.

CHAPTER FOUR

JAMES waited a few seconds. 'Does Richard plan to come back?'

'Here?' Tessa's startled eyes flew to his face. 'No. No, I don't think so. Not for me, I mean. Perhaps, some day. . .to work. I don't know. He didn't find it easy here towards the end—he was frustrated. He missed the. . . social life. And he likes what he's doing now.'

'It can't be easy, managing on your own.'

'But I'm not.' She frowned her puzzlement. 'Jean-Paul was here. Now you. This last week is the only time we haven't had a surgeon.'

James was frowning, too. 'I didn't mean for work,' he said deeply. 'I meant for you personally.'

'Oh.' Tessa realised she couldn't have explained things very well in London. 'It isn't just that Richard's gone away,' she told him. 'We've properly separated. The marriage is over. And it isn't so difficult to be. . .on my own,' she added. In fact, she'd barely given a thought to it and now that she did it seemed that her life was infinitely easier without Richard. 'I'm very busy.'

'Will you divorce?'

His eyes were very dark—probing—almost as if her answer was important to him, and she looked back, wondering why it could be. 'I suppose. One day.' She looked away, gathering the precious films together and replacing them in their folder. 'We'd better go and tell Mustaf,' she said briskly.

'We'll amputate here,' James said to Mustaf, drawing an imaginary line across his leg where he'd make the incision. He explained his technique in considerable detail, told him the operation would take about half an hour and looked at Tessa expectantly.

52

'We'll cut your leg tomorrow,' she translated bluntly.

James eyed her doubtfully. 'Explain he'll be in hospital probably four weeks or so,' he said slowly. 'When the leg has healed completely we'll fit him with a prosthesis and teach him how to walk again.'

'God willing, you will get better,' she said flatly, realising that she should have explained the Sadakhi psyche to James before bringing him to the ward. Men like Mustaf were warrior-like—pragmatic and fatalistic. They neither needed nor wanted lengthy explanations.

'After surgery we give Mustaf's leg to his family,' she told him, after they'd finished on the ward. 'For proper burial. When he dies he'll be buried with his leg so he's complete again.'

He looked surprised, but didn't comment. She asked him to wait outside the women's ward while she told them she'd be bringing a male doctor in to see them so that those who wished could cover their faces. Here it was raucous, with children crying and running around and two women in labour. The female relatives who had come with them were wailing at the end behind a curtained partition.

'One of the highest birth rates in the world,' she explained, after they'd finished seeing the women. 'But also one of the highest maternal and infant mortality rates so I'm trying to encourage them either to come here or at least to let one of our nurses be present at their deliveries. At the moment there's still resistance, especially from the older women, the more traditional ones—the husbands' mothers, that is—and those women are all powerful still. But in the ones we do become involved with we're definitely reducing some of the peri-natal problems.'

'Success stories?'

'Loads.' She smiled. 'Twins recently, one difficult breech who would otherwise have died. A couple of post-delivery haemorrhages in the last month who, I'm sure, would have as well. We're making a difference.'

'I can see that.' They were walking towards the mess now and he smiled at her. 'It must be addictive.'

'It is.' She beamed, pleased that he understood. 'We're also sponsoring three other nurses through their training in the capital, and when they return we'll be able to offer a very good service.'

'What about doctors?'

'If we could we would but there are only two schools in this part of the country. Literacy among those aged over fifteen is running at less than twenty per cent, much less, of course, for women.' She skipped ahead of him and opened the mess door. 'Sadakh's infrastructure's been destroyed by war and the education system's more or less defunct outside the capital. And the doctors there won't leave. They consider the rural areas barbaric and dangerous. If they go anywhere it's to Paris or London.'

She'd started making more tea and looked up to see Axel approaching. 'Here's our anaesthetist,' she told James. 'Axel Nordstrom.' She smiled. 'I think you'll like him.'

Because it was Thursday, the eve of the Holy Day in Sadakh, there'd been no surgery or outpatients scheduled for the afternoon and Axel had been in town, purchasing supplies. He burst in with a broad grin, clutching two unplucked scrawny chickens by their feet, his round face flushed with triumph. 'Four sacks of wheat,' he announced, dumping a chicken on a chair while he briefly shook James's hand and nodded a welcome. 'Four sacks of corn, seven kilos of meat and ten litres of oil. And two chickens to welcome our brilliant surgeon. I am a genius. What am I? A genius.'

He dumped the other chicken, squeezed Tessa's cheeks and kissed her, making her squeal.

'It's true,' she told James, laughing, as she saw first his frown, then his guarded expression, while the flamboyant Finn released her and strode about the room, beating his chest. 'He is a genius. He might not be much of an anaesthetist but he's a hell of a negotiator.'

'Not much of an anaesthetist?' Axel howled. 'Woman, you offend me.'

'OK.' She made a face. 'The best anaesthetist in the world,' she said appeasingly.

And Axel looked appeased. 'Perhaps not in the world,' he said modestly. 'Perhaps only this hemisphere.' He eyed James. 'You like chicken?'

'Yes.'

'Then I make my special Finnish chicken Maryland,' said Axel, scooping up the chickens again. 'Rejoice.'

He walked outside, then swivelled back at the door. 'One rule,' he announced. 'Hands away from my beautiful Helena. The others. . .?' He shrugged expressively, glancing at Tessa with mock dismissiveness then grinning at James—a grin which Tessa saw James now returning. 'You can decide. But this one, I think, is too bossy.'

Tessa threw the cleaning sponge at Axel, hissing when he ducked out of its range. 'Ratbag,' she shouted. 'Go pluck your birds and leave us in peace.'

'He gets worse,' she told James, when the sound of the Finn's maniacal chuckles had receded. 'But he's superb at his job. Even Richard had to admit that—' She stopped. Richard and Axel had never got on but that was irrelevant now.

'Richard never liked anybody else being the centre of attention,' James said shrewdly.

'Perhaps.' Avoiding his eyes, she passed him the tea she'd finished preparing. 'Try it,' she insisted when he hesitated. 'It's different to the one I made this morning. There are hundreds of different teas here.'

It was late now and she realised that the others must have eaten lunch while she and James had been working because she found two covered plates in the kitchen next door. Too hungry to bother reheating the food, she served it immediately. Rice, a little curried lamb and some spicy spinach, the food was delicious but she was surprised to see James eat it with an appreciation that suggested near-starvation.

His helping was much larger but they finished at the same time and she raised her eyebrows. 'Good?'

'I haven't eaten since a sandwich this time yesterday at Heathrow,' he said ruefully. 'There was a strike at the Air France kitchens, nothing except tea at the airport last night and obviously the small planes didn't serve anything.'

To add to her guilt, she stood to clear the plates and saw James's bags still in the corner of the mess. 'Oh, heavens!' she squeaked. 'I've starved you, served you tea that made you gag, then pushed you around the hospital for hours and I haven't even shown you where you'll be staying. What a hotel. No wonder no one ever comes back.'

'Stop worrying.' His grin was lazy. 'The plane's left. I'm stuck here now.'

'Nevertheless. . .'

He collected his bags and, unable to stop herself, she stroked the soft leather appreciatively. 'How much did these cost?'

'I'm not going to tell you.' He followed her into the corridor, steady where she found herself skipping. 'And you've never actually told me how much you're paying me for this job.'

'Stop complaining,' she said cheerfully, whirling to poke her tongue out at him. 'Enjoy the mystery.'

She stopped at the door next to hers and pushed it open to reveal a small, pale room containing a single wooden bed, a rail for him to hang his clothes and a battered filing cabinet which doubled as a dresser. The room faced east and she'd left the shutters open, hoping that the view of the purple-blue peaks that soared behind the barren hills would distract him from the drabness of the room.

James walked to the window and looked out, lingering a few seconds before slowly turning around. 'The view is sublime,' he said softly, 'but something tells me I've been lured here on false promises.'

'Sorry.' She smiled. 'When we spoke on the radio I might have exaggerated a little.'

'I did wonder.' He smiled back. ' "Five-star luxury. *En suite*. Room service. Mini-bar"?'

'My words exactly, I suspect.' And then she laughed. 'I was joking, you knew that. But there is room service.' She banged on the wall with her fist. 'Do this and I'll bring you tea. How about that?'

'You're next door?' At her nod, he said softly, 'That could be fun.'

'It'll be great,' she agreed. 'I promise you tea any hour of the day or night.'

'What if I told you it isn't tea I'm interested in?'

'Tea's all that's on offer,' she said lightly, feeling herself start to tingle.

'Pity.' James tilted his head, regarding her speculatively. 'Richard is definitely out of the picture, isn't he, Tessa?'

'Out of the country, even,' she said breathlessly, wondering.

'Then. . .?'

'Then nothing.' She smiled, realising that despite her self-consciousness with him she wouldn't be able to help but enjoy herself with James. Although she knew he was only teasing, it had been years since anybody had flirted with her, and certainly no one ever had with the skill to make her pulse flutter the way it was doing now. 'You don't waste any time,' she said lightly.

'Perhaps I've just decided what I want.'

'No, James.'

'You don't sound very sure.'

'Oh, but I am. Positive.' She laughed. 'You're indescribably gorgeous, you know. Do women ever resist you?'

'Not usually.' His eyes narrowed. 'Does that mean you're going to try?'

'Your ego doesn't need any boosting from me.'

'We'll talk about that one day.' Then he smiled. 'There's no bathroom here. Do I share yours?'

'Of course. You and Helena and Axel and Monique all use mine.'

'Cosy.' He crouched over one of his bags and the easy movement drew her attention to the powerful strength of his thighs. 'I'll take a shower now before the rush.'

'Jacuzzi and sauna at the end of the hall,' she said, smiling. 'Check your key with the attendant and he'll give you hot towels.'

'I bet.' Standing now, he tucked a finger beneath her chin and tilted her head up to him. 'Hot running water? Luxurious bubble-bath?'

'Sorry.' She stifled a giggle at the sudden vision of James, complete with floral bath hat, immersed in bubbles. Then she visualised James, just James, powerfully male—without the hat or bubbles—and sobered.

'You'll find a barrel of cold water and a bucket,' she said abruptly, stepping back to direct him towards the bathroom. 'And don't use the bubble bath. It's Monique's. It's very precious to her.'

'I'll remember that.'

She went back to the wards for the few hours before dinner, and as she walked over towards the mess she could smell Axel's chickens cooking and her stomach sank.

But Mohammed caught her up before she could reach the building. 'A baby,' he panted. 'There's a baby sick. They need you.'

Tessa sprinted back to the women's ward, shoving the curtain across and dashing into the maternity area. The baby, lying between her weeping mother's thighs, was still but she was becoming pinker with each breath, although her legs and arms were dusky.

One of the nurses, Karima, sucked gently on a piece of tubing to clear the infant's airway and then she breathed into the child's nose, holding the oxygen mask

above her little head. 'Cord around the neck,' she said
between breaths. 'I freed it but she was still dark.'

Tessa stood back, letting her continue, and stroked
the mother's hand. 'It's all right,' she whispered. 'It's
all right.'

And she was right. Within seconds the baby spluttered,
shifted and let out a vigorous cry. Keeping the mask
close to her face, Karima passed her over to her mother
who began to rock her.

'I wanted you there, just in case,' Karima said quietly,
her face flushed and excited.

'You did wonderfully.' Tessa toyed with the baby's
limbs as her mother rocked her, pleased at their strength
and the vigorousness of the baby's pout when she tickled
her cheek.

In London, she reflected—James's presence in Sadakh
reminding her of that distant place—she'd have handled
that very differently. But Karima was well trained for
conditions here and the experience was important for her.
'Well done.'

She washed, checked the baby again properly and
returned to the mess.

James and Helena were immersed in a chess game and
looked up only briefly to acknowledge her.

Monique was curled up in the easy chair, wearing,
Tessa noted, her best dress—a brief, floral shift
she hadn't seen her in since Richard had left. She was
watching the other two with a faint petulance that
worried Tessa.

Living and working so closely together, there were
always going to be occasional disagreements within the
group, but serious discord could rip them apart. And
although she knew that Helena was in love with Axel
she knew also that Helena enjoyed teasing Monique.
And the way she was laughing with James was certainly
doing that.

'Check. Checkmate.' A few minutes later James eased

his chair back, acknowledging the nurse's good-natured protests with a grin.

'Best of three,' Helena said. 'I'll get you tomorrow.'

'No.' Monique looked more lively now. 'It's my turn now and tomorrow. Only I don't know how to play. James, will you teach me?'

'Not now.' James stood up, rubbing the back of his head, and then he looked at Tessa and she saw no tiredness, only a vivid intensity that enervated her. 'Axel says dinner's not till nine. Come for a walk?'

'Yes.' A walk with James, she decided, was exactly what she wanted.

Ignoring Helena's wink and Monique's sulky expression, she walked ahead of him into the night. 'Hospital by night grand tour,' she teased, tucking her hand into the warm crook of his elbow. Cool now, the night air was crisp and refreshing against her heated cheeks. 'Glamour, tension, excitement.'

'Darkness.' He caught her when she stumbled on a rock. 'Fireworks.'

Tessa stiffened, seeing the red-pink trail he'd noticed. The air was silent, apart from the sound of their electricity generator on the other side of the hospital, and the tracer fire far away. It couldn't be near Mustaf's village—must be random fire from the hills. 'Snakes, spiders and scorpions,' she added cheerfully, stamping her feet to scare any such creatures away, as they walked towards the perimeter. 'Mines, flame-throwers, rockets and mortar shells.'

'Oh.' James stopped, forcing her to halt too. 'Not fireworks.'

'Hardly.' In the starlight she could see his face but not his expression, although she suspected that he was scowling, and she smiled. 'But good guess for a rookie.'

'Witch.' But he laughed. 'You're patronising me.'

'It'll do you good.' She was laughing, too, now. 'You're far too sure of yourself, James Hyatt. But you're in my country now. Out here I'm boss.'

'Are you, now?' His voice was rough—it rasped against her skin. He swung her around, capturing the hand she lifted to defend herself. 'You sound pretty sure of yourself.'

'I am.' Her voice sounded breathy. 'I like giving the orders.'

'Really?' He tugged her a few inches closer. They were far from the light of the buildings and his hands were warm on her arms and the darkness was suddenly intimate and she could smell the soapy freshness of his skin. 'You smell nice.'

'So do you.' She chewed at her lower lip, not liking the way he was making her insides turn to liquid. 'James, I don't think this is a good—'

'Yes, it is. It's a very good idea. In fact, it's the best idea I've had in months.' And the darkness became more pronounced as his head blocked the stars, and then he was kissing her.

She pressed her lips together, fighting the temptation of his embrace, but he was big and strong. He twined his right hand in her hair and gripped her, his left hand at her back, forcing her still as he coaxed her—working her lips slowly apart until with a softly bemused groan she surrendered, and he possessed her mouth, making nonsense of her assertion that she was boss.

His tongue ravished her, seduced her then teased her sweetly, lightly, until she wanted to scream. She clutched at him, her fingers digging into his shoulders, and then, slowly, he lifted his head. Both hands were buried in her hair and he was breathing fast. 'You're delicious.' He kissed her again, briefly now. Hard. Determined. 'I want to eat you.'

She was weak but she fought. 'No.'

'Why not?' He kissed her again, or she kissed him— she couldn't tell which, only that it was glorious and she revelled in it.

But still she hated herself for her weakness and finally she wrenched her head away, barely able to breathe.

'You're not playing fair.' She pulled back, then buried her forehead against his chest lest he saw somehow through the darkness how much he'd dazed her. Which was ridiculous, she thought weakly. That much must be blindingly obvious.

'I never promised "fair".' His voice was very deep— it rumbled between them. 'Why are you fighting this?'

'Because. . .just because. I thought you were playing. Pretending. Before.'

'I never pretend.'

Suddenly she heard the adult male intent in his voice and she stiffened, then carefully pulled herself away, realising she'd underestimated his seriousness. 'James. . .no.'

'Why, Tessa?' He tugged her back and his hand slid to her breast and cupped it through her clothes, making her shudder.

But she spun away from him. 'I mean it.' She crossed her arms across her chest, tensing in case he was angry. But he said nothing, and after a few moments she turned back, mustering a pale smile. 'You're quite a kisser,' she said, hoping he'd react calmly to her miserable attempt at humour. 'Talk about knocking my socks off.'

'It's not your socks that particularly interest me,' he said dryly.

And then she could hear someone calling and they both looked up. In the distant lights from the mess she could see Monique's silhouette, and she was calling them urgently to dinner.

'Coming!' Tessa ran one still-trembling hand through her short hair, and then looked at James again. 'We'd better go.'

'Yes.' To her surprise, James tucked her other hand back inside his arm. 'I want you,' he said, almost conversationally.

She stopped, suddenly, and faced him, bracing herself. This was the right time to end this. 'Look, James, you're very attractive,' she said bluntly. 'Incredibly attractive, in fact. And I'm sure you'd be a very good lover, only I don't think I'd be very good at playing those sorts of games and I don't want to get involved like that. Not ever again.'

'We'll talk,' he said, not sounding particularly concerned. 'Let's go. Chicken smells good.'

She frowned, knowing she only had herself to blame if he didn't take her seriously. She probably sounded silly to him. She'd said no, true, but she hadn't exactly resisted his kisses. What she'd said about him knocking her socks off had been true. She tilted her head. 'I am serious.'

'So am I.' He took her arm again. 'Is Axel a good cook?'

'Awful.' She stared up at him. 'His food's inedible. James, when I say no that's it. No. Totally no. No arguments.'

'I hear you.'

They were in the light now, and she saw nothing in his face but quiet calm but, having sensed his determination, that wasn't particularly reassuring.

The others had already started eating and Tessa ignored Helena's and Mohammed's speculative stares and Monique's stony look, concentrating instead on the dish Axel had prepared.

As usual with Axel, it smelled interesting but Tessa knew enough to be wary and she dished herself a very small helping of the chicken, filling her plate with rice. She poured herself a large glass of water.

But James, despite her warning, had no inhibitions about the size of his serving, and he dished himself a huge plateful of the chicken, adding only a small spoonful of rice. 'Looks good,' he said heartily.

'Water?' Tessa held up the jug, giving him a meaningful look, but he waved the water aside, and she didn't insist.

She put a forkful of rice in her mouth and waited,

seeing that Helena, Monique and Mohammed were all doing the same thing.

To James's credit, he didn't choke or spit it out. In fact, although his jaw tightened, he managed to swallow. This time he didn't protest when Tessa passed him the water, taking it and pouring himself one glass and then another—although she didn't look at him again, worried she'd laugh out loud.

'Not too long a list for Saturday,' she told Axel, to distract him in case he looked at James. He was thin-skinned about his cooking and she didn't want his feelings hurt. 'Although there's a bit of action outside so anything might happen.'

'Doing Mustaf?' Helena sounded as if she was trying not to laugh herself.

'Yes. James agrees.' She took another mouthful of rice. 'A straightforward above knee amputation will have him out of here within a month. It makes sense. What do you think, Axel?'

'Whatever.' He beamed as he helped himself to more chicken. 'Gas 'em and clear 'em—that's my motto.'

Mohammed watched Axel tuck into his chicken, his expression kindly bemused. Normally a healthy eater, tonight Mohammed had only managed a small helping. 'Was the baby all right?'

'She'd had the cord around her neck,' Tessa explained. It was becoming obvious that she was eating only rice and she steeled herself for a bite of the chicken. 'She was fine. Karima resuscitated her; she just wanted me to check her out.'

'Karima's very good.' Helena took more rice. 'She loves the work.'

'We're lucky to have her.' Tessa's throat was burning from the tiny morsel of chicken she'd managed and she stuffed her mouth with rice, then drank water quickly. James was watching her, she saw, his blue eyes sparkling, but she looked away immediately and wished she'd not made her own enjoyment at his first reaction so obvious.

'I can't finish this.' Monique was the first to push her plate away. 'I'm too full from lunch.' She turned to James. 'We could go for a walk, if you want. I could show you the constellations.' She eyed Tessa through her lashes. 'Richard taught me some of them. I will teach you.'

Tessa tensed slightly at the mention of her husband, forcing a small smile when James looked at her.

'Another time,' he said casually to Monique, although he was watching Tessa, his expression enigmatic.

Helena stood up suddenly. 'I'm full, too,' she declared, swiftly gathering up her own plate and Monique's, and scooping Tessa's away too—holding them high so Axel wouldn't notice how much chicken was left.

'I'll take these.' Tessa swept up James's and Mohammed's plates, and followed Helena to the kitchen where they both dissolved into laughter.

'Did you see James's face?' Helena demanded, her eyes streaming. 'I thought he was going to burst.'

'I couldn't look.' Tessa collapsed against the bench, almost crying. 'God! That was the worst. Helena, you've got to say something.'

'I can't,' the nurse wailed. 'He tries so hard. You tell him.'

'I tried.' Her sides were aching now and Tessa held her stomach. 'But he was so hurt by me just making a tiny suggestion that I chickened out. We can't keep going through this every week. We have to stop him.'

'Can James cook?'

'I don't know. I hope so.' The hospital cook didn't cook for them either the night before the Holy Day or on the Holy Day itself, and although they took turns at preparing meals on one of the evenings Axel, who enjoyed cooking, always cooked the other.

The door opened and James stood there with the empty rice dish and the bowl of chicken. 'You set me up,' he said softly to Tessa, his eyes scanning their tear-stained faces.

'I tried to warn you.' She was laughing again. 'Axel can't smell and he's barely got any taste. He can't tell how bad it is.'

'No smell?' James looked astounded. 'He's an anaesthetist. What about the gases?'

'He works closely with his anaesthetic nurses,' she explained. 'He was in a car crash ten years ago and had a head injury. He lost his sense of smell.'

'But he loves to cook,' Helena added. 'And he is sensitive. We cannot criticise him.'

Tessa said eagerly, 'Can you cook? None of us can. You could say you love it. You could beg to split the nights with him.'

'Only if you don't mind scrambled eggs and omelettes,' James said ruefully.

'Oh, dear.' Helena gathered the dishes into a big steel sink and topped it up with boiling water from the kettle and detergent. 'Never mind.'

Tessa refilled the kettle and put it back on the gas to boil for tea. She looked up and caught James yawning. 'Go to bed,' she told him. 'There's only tea and you don't like it, anyway.'

'I will.' His eyes were very dark. 'Come with me?'

'No.'

'Pity.'

Helena laughed her delight as he left, smothering the sound as she met Tessa's affronted glare.

CHAPTER FIVE

TESSA wasn't disturbed during the night and woke at five to the distant sounds of the morning call to prayer drifting from the mosque in the town. For a few seconds she lay still, enjoying the chilly pre-dawn darkness, and then she sprang out of bed and hurried to the bathroom.

After bathing and dressing in jeans and a plain shirt, she knocked on James's door. Although still early, it was light now and she thought he might like to go for a drive around the local area while the air was soft and cool. There was no reply and she pushed it open. 'James. . .'

But the room was empty, the bed already made, the room tidy.

She found him in the mess, reading one of the papers he'd brought. His hair damp so he'd obviously also bathed, and he looked up when she walked in. 'I've been to the wards and nothing's brewing,' he said easily. 'There's toast made in the kitchen and water boiled for tea.'

'My.' Tessa was impressed. And grateful. Richard and Jean-Paul had both been hard to move in the morning, and the job of getting them both up and working had invariably fallen to her. 'I think I love you.'

'That's a start.' Grinning, he waved an arm to get rid of her. 'Get some breakfast and let's go. I want to see this place.'

'We'll go to the town,' she said when she returned with half a toasted roll, thickly coated with some of the precious peanut butter he'd brought from London. 'It'll be quiet since there's no market today, but that'll make it easier to move around.'

Before they left she donned a long white *chaderi* which covered her completely, a narrow grid of netting the only

67

concession to allow her to see. James was waiting in the Jeep, and he stared at her, clearly aghast, when she hiked it up and clambered in beside him.

'It's best,' she explained. 'I don't want to offend anyone.'

'Won't they be curious about why you're with a European?'

'Hardly.' Tessa laughed. The garment was long and cumbersome and she invariably managed to trip over her feet at least once. 'I stomp around like a lame horse in this but the local women look like they're gliding. Watch them—they're very graceful. Everyone can tell I'm foreign.'

She directed him out onto the road, reminding him to drive on the right, although—given the narrow width of the track—that was hardly relevant. She explained how important it was that he kept to the well-worn rutted area. 'There are thousands of mines buried around here and the road's the only strip that's been cleared. One inch off. . .' she clapped her hands dramatically '. . .and boom!'

'Thanks.' James lifted his eyes briefly to the sky. 'That's useful. Any more handy hints?'

'Hundreds,' she said airily. 'I am a mine of information.'

They parked near the main market-place. Normally lined with colourful stalls and crowds, this morning the ancient square would be less crowded—but today it was unusually quiet. One small boy with four wayward goats and two men, drinking tea beneath a huge walnut tree, were the only visitors apart from themselves.

The buildings around the square were white-stained mud brick. Shambolic yet picturesque, the ones which had been most severely damaged by the war remained unrepaired, their pock-marked façades crumbling and decayed.

'More than two hundred people died in this place at the height of the fighting,' Tessa explained quietly. 'The soldiers forced them to line up in rows there. . .' she indicated the scarred wall that made up the north boundary of the square '. . .and shot them. Then they raided and looted street by street, shooting anyone not quick enough to run away, until the town was empty.'

'What happened to all the people?'

'Luckily, a lot of those not involved in the fighting had already gone. To the capital or to relatives in distant villages. Those who were left and not injured or dead fled into the desert, returning later when the rebels regained control.'

'Were you here when this happened?'

'Richard and I were in the capital. We heard about the massacre and chartered a plane to bring us here. We arrived three days after the shootings. There were many, many injuries, more than a hundred people needing surgery. As well as Richard, we had two other surgeons at that stage, a handful of nurses and aides and only the most basic of facilities. The hospital here had been looted and bits of it had been destroyed by fire, making much of the building too risky to work in, hence the reason we had to use tents. We operated day and night for so long I can hardly remember.'

'And then you stayed.'

'Even if we'd wanted to—which we didn't—we couldn't have left. There were no others to take our places. When the war ended we built where we are now, thinking the facility might attract workers back to the area, but then the civil fighting started and there's never really been peace here.'

They were strolling around the dusty, tiled square. 'Some of the young people whose lives we saved then have now grown up, and they bring their children to us. They trust us. We've been able to start immunisation programmes and water purification schemes. If we left that would all fall apart.'

'Is it healthy to encourage that sort of dependence?' he asked gravely.

Tessa hesitated, then remembered that she'd taunted him with exactly the same words in London. 'We're trying to change things,' she said lightly. 'We're trying to train others.'

They rounded a corner, and she stopped. Ahead of them, perhaps a hundred yards away, a group of uniformed soldiers lounged around a darkly tinted Mercedes. Another group, smaller—and wearing blue instead of khaki—but as heavily armed, guarded a broad, fortified building across the street. A tank squatted in the street between them and the atmosphere was tense.

James stopped when she did, and he frowned at her, obviously sensing her unease. 'Army?'

'Militia. Their bosses must be meeting.' Tessa backed away warily, then turned back into the square out of sight. 'Not the best street to choose for a stroll,' she said carefully. 'Let's go back to the Jeep.

'When the Russians retreated they left a lot of their military hardware behind in return for being allowed out alive. The men who took the equipment became very powerful—warlords, literally. There are four in this area, each with his own army, equipment, weapons. They form alliances occasionally but they're always fragile, and the fighting creates the anarchy that is endemic in Sadakh now. The government mounts periodic incursions into their territories but never properly gains control because the warlords control the arms and the opium trade here— and thus the money.'

'And the groups we saw?'

'Traditional rivals,' Tessa explained. 'The troops by the car come from villages north-east of here. The fighting from the hills, the missiles that are fired at our planes and the bombs probably come from them. They're fighting for total control of the region but, really, it's a terrorist war that they wage.'

'It's good, then, that these two groups are talking.'

'I don't know.' It was after nine now and the sun was growing hot, but the square was still very quiet and that worried her, too. She veered towards the Jeep, shooing away the ragged chickens that clucked softly under it. 'This doesn't feel right. Let's get out of here.'

She took James on a tour of the rest of the town, after which they visited two of the local villages, stopping now and then to speak with people she knew and introduce them to their new surgeon.

Back at the hospital over lunch she told Axel and Mohammed about the militia they'd seen in the town.

Both men expressed the same surprise she'd felt. 'Let us hope that this is a peaceful meeting,' Mohammed murmured cautiously, 'and not a council of war.'

'No one was smiling,' Tessa said quietly.

'Then that may be very bad,' said Mohammed with a sigh.

'Ah, death.' Axel, always optimistic, was grinning. 'The afterlife. At last, the mystery solved.'

'Idiot.' Tessa rolled her eyes, although inwardly she was worried. The two groups they'd seen meeting were the most powerful in the region. 'We are safe here,' she said slowly. They'd weathered conflict not only in the general area but in the town itself before, without becoming involved. 'Everyone knows the hospital's run by foreigners and we've agreed to treat only civilians. We've been careful never to take sides.'

'Which means you've bribed everyone?' enquired James, surprising her with his astuteness. It had taken her months to acquire that sort of cynicism.

'Broadly speaking,' she admitted.

'Broadly, nothing.' Axel wagged a scolding finger at her. 'That is it exactly, James. We survive while we pay. It is a token, of course, of respect but it's that simple.'

'Remind me to write you another cheque,' James muttered, making her smile.

She pushed her plate away. 'I'll go and check the wards. Helena says there're a few things for me to see.'

'I'll come with you.' James followed her out. 'I've

been thinking about this. I should cover the men, plus the women's and children's surgical.'

'That's how I worked it with Jean-Paul,' she said, nodding thanks for his offer. Sharing that way would diminish her workload considerably, leaving her more time for training local staff and running her preventative medicine programmes. 'Axel helps with the medical side of things, as well as anaesthetics, and he's superb with pain management—not that we have a wide range of choices. We usually cover outpatients together.'

She stopped at a small supply room which doubled as their pharmacy and unlocked it for him to inspect. 'Pain relief is basically paracetamol, codeine, one of the opiate drugs like morphine or a simple non-steroidal,' she said, showing him their supplies. 'Antibiotics—the usual ones. We still mostly use the basics—penicillin, Flagyl, gentamicin, and so on. Here are the tuberculosis drugs we have and a few more exotic anti-infection agents.

'Over here are the malarial drugs, the anti-diarrhoeals and rehydration solutions—infant and adult.' She opened the gas-powered fridge that housed the vaccines for immunisations. 'Sodium heparin and human insulin.'

James nodded. 'Anaesthetics?'

'In Theatre. All anaesthetic equipment, including local, is kept there, as well as a small supply of antibiotics, some analgesics and most of the emergency drugs.'

'Oxygen?'

'We have our own compressor. Tanks on the wards and in Theatre. Mohammed keeps track of supplies and organises refills.'

'Blood?'

'In the lab.' She ushered him out of the office and took him to their laboratory. A small but purpose-built room, the lab contained a Bunsen burner, a sink, a shelf which held their chemicals, a microscope and a fridge. 'We have a good technician and another who's learning the job, but there'll still be times when you'll find it quicker to look at a blood film or a urine yourself. We don't have a full pathology service by any means, but there is some basic staining equipment if you want to experiment.'

'Real medicine.'

'Isn't it?' She smiled. 'How long since you ventured inside a lab?'

'About fifteen years,' he admitted wryly.

'I'm happy to demonstrate things but you'll find it all comes back fairly easily when you start. In fact, I like playing around in here. It's fun.'

'I'm not sure that's quite the right word.' He followed her out, waiting while she locked the room. 'Anything you can't do, Tessa Mathesson?'

She laughed. 'Am I intimidating you?'

'Of course.' He patted her back lightly as they walked along the corridor. 'Isn't that the idea?'

'Maybe just a little.' She suspected it didn't happen to him very often and she knew it wouldn't happen for long here. As soon as he began operating their roles would become reversed.

She took him to see a patient Axel had seen during the day and admitted. A thirty-year-old man, he lay quiet and deeply yellow on his bed. He described a short history of jaundice and several days of intensely itchy skin.

While Tessa translated for James, Fazal sat forward so they could see his back, demonstrating the scratches he'd made with his fingers in a fruitless battle to get relief from the itching.

'Urine?' Tessa asked. 'Stool?'

'Urine dark like the night. Stool pale as sand,' he told them.

He'd felt increasingly unwell over the past week although, significantly, none of his family had shared any of his symptoms and he'd not been in contact with anybody with jaundice. That made hepatitis a less likely diagnosis.

But the striking feature in his history was the day he'd had of pain and fever and shaking and this, together with the tenderness Axel had noted over his liver, suggested acute infection in the duct system draining his liver and gall-bladder, most likely secondary to something blocking part of the duct.

Axel had admitted him for intravenous hydration and antibiotics, with a view to surgery.

'Ascaris worms probably blocking the bile ducts,' Tessa said to James, holding up the temperature chart to demonstrate the fever and realising it would not be a condition he was particularly familiar with. 'They're roundworms. Very common in this part of the world. We had a similar case a month ago.'

James sat on the edge of the bed and gently examined their patient's abdomen, confirming Axel's earlier findings. 'I can't feel his gall-bladder,' he said quietly. 'Surgery tomorrow.'

'I agree.' Tessa told their patient they would operate the following day. 'If it is roundworms we inject antibiotic into the duct and duodenum,' she explained, 'otherwise the worms can work their way through the suture lines and into the peritoneum.'

'Nasty.' He studied her. 'Does everybody carry them?'

'Virtually universal,' she confirmed. 'We routinely treat for them.' She smiled. 'You'll probably pick them up, too,' she said lightly. 'We've all been dosed.'

'Looking forward to it,' he said dryly. 'Thanks.'

After finishing with Fazal, she left him at the men's ward with Mohammed to translate so that he could see the rest of their male patients. She wanted to check the maternity patients and the baby from last night, if she was still an inpatient, before she did anything. 'If I don't see you on the wards I'll see you at dinner.'

'What?' Grey-blue eyes regarded her gravely. 'No pre-dinner walk?'

Tessa resisted the impulse to poke her tongue out at him, deciding that the gesture was too childish and one she should stop using. 'I don't think so,' she said carefully, determined not to blush. 'Ask Monique—she might be interested.'

James stilled. 'Thank you for the advice,' he said formally, his eyes unreadable now. 'I'll give it due consideration.'

'Good.' She lifted her chin and walked away quickly, angry with herself for letting his reply bother her.

Dinner that evening was subdued. Mohammed and the other staff who sometimes dined with them had gone home to be with their families. Axel had one of the headaches to which he was prone, and Helena spent most of the meal clucking about him sympathetically. Monique was sulkily quiet and, judging from the resentful stares Tessa was receiving, James had not elected to invite her for an evening stroll.

James himself was quiet, too, and although she caught him looking at her a little broodingly at times he barely spoke.

Afterwards Tessa retreated to her office and spent the evening doing administrative work. When she returned to the mess hours later only one lamp was still lit. James sat beneath it, an unopened book in one hand, and when she walked in he looked directly at her, his gaze shadowed.

'Everything all right?' he said quietly.

She nodded. 'I haven't been on the wards but no one's called me. I've been doing paperwork.' She sat beside him and curled her legs beneath her. 'What are you reading?'

'Tolstoy.' He smiled at her expression. 'Confession. I haven't started yet.'

'Confession.' She smiled back. 'I've never even seen the TV series.'

'Are you a reader?'

'I used to be.' She pulled her shoes off and let them drop to the floor. She flexed her toes. 'Before I started university I read every day. After that I seemed to get out of the habit.'

'I know the feeling.' He swung her feet around and then lifted them onto his lap, tugging her socks free before beginning to massage her soles with strong, warm hands. 'Too many textbooks to study.'

'True.' She lay back, sighing appreciatively. 'That's nice.'

'Good.'

'I shouldn't be letting you do this.'

'Indulge me.' His hands moved firmly up and down her feet, first her left, then her right, kneading her flesh. 'You have lovely feet.'

She closed her eyes. This was bliss. No one had ever massaged her feet before—she'd had no idea it would feel so good. 'I've got funny toes.'

'Beautiful toes.'

'Too short.'

'Just the right size.'

She felt like purring. 'I could go to sleep.'

Halfway there, she made an effort to resist. 'But I mustn't.' Reluctantly she forced one eye open. 'I'll wake up all stiff and cold. I have to go to bed.'

'I'll keep you warm.'

'No.' Flushing now, she braced her hand against the back of the couch and prepared to swing herself around.

But before she could move his hand slid up her leg, then beneath her and he lifted her. 'I'll take you to your bed.'

'James. . .?'

'Shh.' He carried her easily, as if her weight were nothing. 'You'll wake the others.'

It felt good in his arms and, soothed from the massage, she relaxed, feeling safe. Secure. Then he opened her door and the moon shone in through her open shutters. She saw his face and the glitter in his eyes.

'James, put me down.'

'Stop worrying so.' He lowered her to the bed.

'You're trying to seduce me.'

'Of course I am.' But his smile was soft and he withdrew to the door. 'But not tonight. Sleep well.'

Her eyes were already closed. 'Goodnight.'

Tessa rose early as usual next morning, but once again James had beaten her to the mess.

'Full breakfast today,' he said, gesturing to the plate of gruel their cook had obviously prepared for him.

'Nice, isn't it?' Tessa avoided the gruel, contenting herself with a thick spoonful of peanut butter direct from the jar. Ignoring James's mock disgust at her unorthodox breakfast, she enjoyed the thick spread then poured herself a cup of dark tea. 'Sleep well?'

'Intermittently.' His eyes probed hers. 'You?'

'Nothing ever disturbs me,' she said cheerfully. 'I thought I'd take you round the patients on your list this morning—'

'Seen them all. Mohammed was around—he translated for me. I've had to switch the order around a little because the child was given some rice this morning by mistake. I've changed her to third. Everything else is fine.'

'Good.' Tessa blinked, vaguely bemused. 'What time did you get up?'

'Early.' He passed her the sugar. 'Are you coming to Theatre?'

'I'd like to, if I'm not too busy. I'm eager to see the master at work.'

James's mouth twitched. 'Your words?'

'Richard's.' She swallowed some of her tea. 'And Delia Buttrose-Allen's.' She smiled. 'She showed me the marvellous job you did on her veins.'

'Hmm.' His eyes narrowed as if he suspected she was mocking him and she was, she acknowledged, about the veins—but only a little. And Richard's admiration was genuine. He'd practically hero-worshipped James, professionally speaking, and—given her husband's egocentricity and his own considerable surgical talent—that was the highest praise he could have bestowed.

Helena and Axel walked in. The anaesthetist was flexing his fingers. 'Today you learn how it feels to work with a true genius,' Axel said to James. 'I hope you are prepared.'

James grinned. 'I'm looking forward to it.'

'I also.' Axel sat beside him, blinking his thanks for the tea Tessa passed before sending her a pained look. 'I'm tired of working with amateurs.'

'Wretch.' But Tessa laughed. She gulped the rest of her drink, then mock-swiped him across the head on her way past. 'You loved playing the back-seat expert. Admit it.'

'I suffered for my craft,' he said feelingly.

'Eat your breakfast.' A smiling Helena dumped a laden plate of gruel in front of him. 'Tessa, OK if I meet you in Children's in ten minutes?'

Tessa nodded, already halfway out the door.

By the time she had an hour spare to visit Theatres it was already late morning. Mustaf and the child who'd been third on the list were awake in Recovery and James was halfway through the day's cases.

He was scrubbing and his blue eyes gleamed at her above his mask. 'If you've some free time you should scrub up. It's Fazal. It might be interesting.'

She joined him as he was about to make the incision and Monique, who was scrub nurse for him, wordlessly passed her a swab. Tessa held back the edges of the wound as he incised steadily down to the peritoneum, the membrane that contained the abdominal contents.

There wasn't a lot of ooze but James paused to buzz the few vessels which were still bleeding before he caught the peritoneum between the artery forceps which Tessa held up, tenting the abdominal membrane so that James could pierce it without worrying about damaging the bowel beneath.

'Since we can't be sure what we'll find, I'm starting with this size,' he said, and she nodded understandingly. In London they'd have had access to tests which would have demonstrated the cause of Fazal's jaundice and probably have allowed them either to avoid surgery by using equipment they didn't have here or else to make a smaller incision in the same place, just under his rib-cage. Here, though, they couldn't be sure of the cause so he needed as much exposure as possible, hence the larger incision.

Despite this being his first session with an unfamiliar team, James worked quickly and fluently and Tessa began to understand the reasons for Richard's admiration.

Yellow-stained fluid bubbled up and Tessa reached for the metal rod at her side. 'Shall I suction?'

'Swab first.' James dabbed with gauze attached to long forceps then leaned forward so she had to draw back lest their heads touched as his right hand probed their patient's liver. 'Congested liver, but I can't feel any other abnormalities,' he said with satisfaction, meeting her eyes as he withdrew his hand. 'The trouble must be in the duct.'

He inserted a self-retaining retractor, which held back the edges of the abdomen, and they swapped places so she could hold back the liver for him, using another retractor in her left hand. 'How does it look?'

'Messy.' He took her retractor so she could bend forward and look. 'The duct's swollen near the liver and there's a narrowing, probably caused by inflammation, near the duodenum.'

She nodded. The narrowing of the duct between the liver and gall-bladder and the duodenum was obvious, and explained why the bile had backflowed into the liver and caused Fazal's jaundice. 'What will you do?'

'First clear the duct,' he said, returning the retractor to her and taking the moist swab Monique had prepared. 'Then try and dilate the stricture and stick a hollow plastic stent in to keep it open. If the damage has been caused by gallstones I'll take the gall-bladder out as well to try and stop recurrence.'

But when he opened the duct it wasn't gallstones which

were causing the problem but, as Tessa had suspected, a tangle of coiled worms, the sort that almost always contaminated the bowels of Sadakhi patients. He tugged them free of the duct and dropped the bile-stained mess into one of the stainless-steel bowls on Monique's trolley.

'Thirty minutes.' Axel looked up from the novel he was reading and peered over them, screwing up his face as he inspected the contents of the bowl. 'Not bad. Finished yet?'

'Hardly.' James stretched the narrowed duct with a smooth metal instrument and inserted a plastic tube into it, which would stay there to hold the duct open. He injected piperazine, an anti-worm drug, either side of the duct and into the duodenum, before suturing the duct closed with fine, neat stitches.

Then he washed out the peritoneum with jugs of warm water, while Tessa suctioned away the slightly murky fluid until it cleared. Then she withdrew her retractor and James released the self-retaining one and replaced the bowel into the cavity.

James looked at her. 'Want to close?'

She shook her head, smiling under her mask. 'Axel's timing,' she said softly. 'He'll complain if I take too long.' But the real reason was that she was enjoying watching him work. She liked watching the fast, accurate way he sutured, which was a world away from her plodding, careful style.

She held up the peritoneum with artery forceps again, releasing them as he sutured and catching the catgut thread he used with her right hand to keep it out of his way. 'You're enjoying yourself.'

'Of course.' Blue eyes twinkled briefly at her. 'Real surgery.'

'Better than varicose veins?'

'This may come as a shock to you but, in fact, I do not spend every session on varicose veins,' he drawled as he knotted his thread. 'I've even been known to tackle the occasional major procedure.'

Tessa laughed as she cut the thread, earning herself a cross glare from Monique, who was just finishing counting her instruments and promptly snapped, 'Count correct.'

'Thanks.' James accepted the local anaesthetic Monique passed to him and infiltrated it into the muscular layers of the wound, then swapped the empty syringe and needle for a skin suture. 'Next patient?'

'On his way.' Axel was fiddling with valves on his anaesthetic machine and he looked up as James tied the first suture into place. 'We'll do the hernia, then break for lunch. That is if that is OK with you, James.'

Tessa looked quickly at Monique and at Helena, who was acting as circulating nurse for the morning, and they both raised their eyebrows, obviously also startled.

Clearly James had impressed Axel this morning—she'd never heard him defer to a surgeon about the timing of lunch before. Even Richard had been forced to stop operating whenever Axel's stomach grumbled.

'Fine, Axel. Any time.' James tied the final stitch, waited for Tessa to cut it, then said, 'Dressing, please.'

'Dressing.' Monique applied gauze to the wound, then taped it in place while Tessa and James unclipped the guards and stripped them.

'Fifty-one minutes, eleven seconds.' Axel whooped his delight. 'At last. A surgeon to match my talents.'

'Jean-Paul was superb in emergencies,' Tessa explained as she and James shed their gloves and untied each other's gowns, 'but he did tend to linger with the routine work, and you can see that Axel has a short attention span.' She bundled her gown into a linen basket. 'Thanks for letting me scrub. I loved watching that. Sure I can't persuade you to spend the rest of your career here?'

'Why don't you try?' He freed his mask. 'I might enjoy it.'

'Staying or the persuasion?' Tessa felt herself starting to flush.

'Oh, the persuasion.' They were alone in the equipment and linen room which adjoined the theatre and suddenly it felt very small and claustrophobic.

'I could offer you money,' she said huskily.

James smiled. Eyes gleaming, he backed her against the shelves which held their suture material until the wood pressed into her back. 'I've got money,' he said softly. 'You have none.'

'Prestige?'

His head tilted slightly. 'Don't need it.'

'Intellectual rewards?'

'Overrated.' He was very close to her now. 'Anything else?'

She put one firm palm against his chest and met his stare with a calmness which belied her shaking legs. 'OK. If it means you'll stay for ever I'll sleep with you.'

There was a short, startled silence and then, as she'd hoped, James laughed. 'Witch.' Her words had dissolved the tension between them and he tugged her forward and pressed a brief, firm kiss to her forehead, before taking himself away. 'Staying for the hernia?'

'Not today.' She returned with him back to Theatre to help the others, wryly noting the pointed stare from Monique that suggested she'd outstayed her welcome. 'Outpatients will be starting.'

James joined her several hours later in the raucous chaos which was Outpatients. He smiled at her. 'Can I be useful?'

'Yes.' She looked up from her patient and beamed at him. 'Helena's around somewhere. She's got a list of people you could see, and she'll translate for you and help out.' She explained to her patient and his mother that James was their new doctor and, in English, said to James, 'Come and feel Ali's tummy. I don't think you'll have seen this in London.'

James examined her patient. He carefully palpated his abdomen, noting his large liver and spleen, then checked underneath the boy's arms, neck and under his eyes.

'Ali is twelve. He's had several months of fever,

tiredness and weight loss,' she explained. 'You see that the skin on his face and abdomen is slightly darkened.'

'Loss of muscle bulk, enlarged lymph nodes, anaemia, enlarged liver and spleen.' James frowned. 'Leishmaniasis?'

'You *have* read my letters.' Tessa smiled her surprise—she hadn't expected him to get the diagnosis right. Few Western doctors recognised the condition when they first arrived. 'You're right, of course. Kala-azar leishmaniasis. Visceral leishmaniasis. Both types—visceral, involving the organs, and cutaneous, where there are ulcerated lesions on the skin—are common here; you'll see a lot.'

'How's it spread?'

'The reservoir is generally man or dogs. Here it's both, and the Sadakhi people love their dogs so we'll probably never change that. Like malaria, the bug's carried by insects—but sandflies this time rather than mosquitoes. It infects white blood cells and damages the blood and marrow and internal organs, especially the liver and spleen.'

'Treatment?'

'We'll admit him for Pentostam intravenously every day for a month, although he can be an outpatient for much of that. That's generally effective. If not there are second-line drugs available. Our cure rate here is good.'

Helena appeared and hauled James away, leaving her alone with her patient and his mother again.

Tessa smiled at Ali. 'We will become good friends,' she said in the local dialect, earning herself a wan smile which, she was confident, would slowly brighten with the treatment.

At the end of the session, once they'd both been to the wards, James joined her for tea in the mess. 'I heard what sounded like a machine-gun firing earlier. What would that have been?'

'I don't know.' She shrugged. She'd heard the firing, too, coming from the edge of town not far away, but it had only lasted a short time and, more importantly, no injuries had been brought to them. 'Could be anything. A death, a celebration, an argument—anything. Firing shots into the air here's like us putting an announcement in *The Times*.'

But, despite her easy reassurance, that evening there was firing from the hills and distant sounds of pounding and one dull boom. Mohammed and Khan, another of their locally trained paramedic staff, joined her and James outside and they watched pink streaks lasering across the moonless sky.

Mohammed said, 'This possibly means yesterday's meeting was not a peaceful one.'

'Or else this is posturing.' Tessa frowned at the sky. 'A last demonstration of power.'

The atmosphere between the four of them was heavy as they returned inside for dinner.

CHAPTER SIX

THE following afternoon Mohammed drove Tessa into town to see Ahmad, the toddler she'd discharged three days before who'd had the mysteriously raised temperature. He still looked well, with no signs of illness, and his buoyant good health reassured her.

But the rest of her visit was worrying. Normally bustling and noisy on such a fine afternoon, the town was quiet, shutters were closed and there were few people on the streets. The market was confined to one side of the square, just a few stalls selling wheat and bread together with a couple of fruit stands displaying peaches and melons.

Normally they would have stopped and bought some of the fruit but there were heavily armed militia at every corner and Mohammed thought it best not to delay.

Twice on the way back to the hospital they were stopped at roadblocks by soldiers, demanding their papers and wanting to search the Jeep. It was not in itself unusual, but this time the soldiers were hostile and uncommunicative, annoyed by her questions where previously she had found them courteous and friendly.

'We'd better start increasing our blood stocks,' she said to Mohammed, turning back to look worriedly at a tank which had stopped behind them at the roadblock. 'Ask all visitors to donate.'

'We have started yesterday.' Mohammed was driving faster than normal. 'I am sending my family away.'

Tessa nodded. Mohammed's home was close to the main square; the precaution was wise. 'You know if you want to go—'

'I stay.' He jolted them across a broad fissure in the road. 'All of us will be needed if there is trouble.'

Late that evening James came and found her in the store-room she used as an office. 'Want a break?'

'Of course.' Gratefully she accepted the tea he'd brought her and pushed her typewriter away. She slid her chair back to make room for him to sit on the edge of her desk.

He grimaced at the sheaf of letters she'd typed. 'Your memoirs?'

'Mohammed's family's leaving for the capital tomorrow.' She smiled. 'Too good an opportunity to miss. I'm giving them all my mail.'

'I'm going to miss your letters.' He tilted his head assessingly. 'Or do I still get one now I'm here?'

'No, you don't.' But she pushed one towards him. 'They'll frighten you,' she said lightly, only she wasn't joking. The letters were frank assessments of the current political instability in the region and contained urgent requests for more equipment—surgical supplies, anti-biotics, burn treatments—the sort of things they'd need desperately if there was an increase in the fighting.

Then there were the basic essentials that had to be covered. 'James, have you made a will?'

'Yes.' He watched her. 'Enjoying your tea?'

She took a hurried sip. 'Mmm.' She hesitated. 'Things aren't good here just now,' she said finally. 'They're unpredictable at best but may get bad. I suppose. . .' she faltered. 'I suppose it wasn't a good time for you to come. Good for us, of course, because we need you, but not for you.'

'There's risk in everything.' He didn't seem perturbed. 'Some would argue that London is dangerous.'

'It's not the same. Me, Axel, Helena, Monique—we all understood the risks involved in coming here and we've chosen to do this work. But you came because you're my friend and I asked for your help. I want you to know that if things start to go badly here I'll get you out.'

'You're seriously worried?'

'I'm trying to be realistic,' she said slowly. 'I don't think we'll be deliberately targeted but that doesn't make us safe.'

He folded his arms. 'Tell me.'

And she did. She explained about the bombing of Mustaf's village, and about how tense the situation was there. And about the roadblocks, and the soldiers' hostility, and the recent noise from the hills when they'd grown used to much less.

It was a relief not to hide anything for she understood that James would listen where Jean-Paul wouldn't have wanted to. And James wouldn't flinch from the truth as Richard might have. Richard, who longed to roam carelessly like a child and for everything to be happy and easy and trouble-free.

When she'd finished his eyes mirrored her concern but his gaze was steady. 'Blood?'

'Organised. The nurses and aides ask every visitor to donate and Mohammed will organise collection in the town.'

'Supplies?'

'Enough at first,' she said. 'More coming if the shipment that's due gets through.'

'Beds?'

'We make do. Mattresses on the floor when we run out, plastic sheets when they're used.'

'Defence?'

'None of our own. Too dangerous.'

'Evacuation plan?'

'Rudimentary.' She grimaced. 'We can move into the desert if the buildings are damaged—use tents again. I. . .I won't want to leave. If the others do they'll have to fly out early if there are major battles. Planes still flew last time even during heavy fighting but it was risky and they might not again. But I'll make sure you get out before anything happens—'

'Don't talk about me,' he interrupted. 'I'm not going anywhere. I came here to do a job.'

She blinked. 'James, you don't understand—'

'I mean it, Tessa.' His expression hadn't changed but suddenly his annoyance was palpable. 'Forget worrying about getting me out because I'm not leaving either.'

'But if something happens to you—'

'You can feel guilty if it pleases you. Not that there'll be any point.' He lifted his hand to stop her as she started to speak. 'Stop it, Tessa.' He sounded exasperated. 'I was well aware of the instability of this place. 'I'm not going to flee at the first sign of trouble just to salve your conscience.'

'Oh.' She wasn't sure what to say. Knowing James, she acknowledged, she should have predicted this.

'I'm not here just for you, Tessa. I'm here for myself as well. I was. . .curious.'

She could understand that. 'It's a fascinating place.'

'Not only about Sadakh.'

'Oh.' She suddenly felt inexplicably breathless. 'About the people, I suppose. And the hospital.'

'Of course. Among other things.'

Tessa looked at the floor. 'Have you satisfied your curiosity?'

'Hardly.' She could feel him studying her. 'It's too soon.'

She looked up quickly, glimpsing something in the dark depths of his eyes that alarmed her. Her whole body stiffened. He hadn't moved from her desk but suddenly he seemed very close. She pushed herself to the back of her chair and shifted her feet so her legs were away from his. 'James. . .?' she whispered uncertainly.

He was still watching her. 'Why not?'

'We've discussed this.'

'No, we haven't. You've told me things—we've discussed nothing.'

'I'm not interested.'

'I understand you're hesitant.' His dark eyes probed hers. 'Your marriage can't have been easy.'

Her breath caught. She shoved the chair back and rose out of it, turning away so he couldn't see her expression. 'That has nothing to do with this.'

'Are you sure you're not still in love with him?'

'Yes. I'm sure.' She stayed stiff. 'I'm not in love with him.'

'Yet you wear his ring.'

'Because rings are important here.' She twirled it on her finger, refusing to turn back. 'They're a symbol, that's all. It makes things easier.'

'Not for me.'

'But, then, I don't want to make things easier for you.' She turned and managed a smile, which he didn't return. 'Come on, James. Lighten up. Try Monique—she'll probably be thrilled.'

'I'm not Richard.'

The words were careful. Careful. Guarded. Wary. But they lingered until she tensed, finally admitting that she understood what he was trying to say. James had been Richard's friend for many years before she'd met them both when they'd all been working at the London so it was hardly surprising he knew. He probably knew Richard as well as she did.

And James was concerned. For her.

'I know everything,' she said quietly. She took a deep breath. 'Richard was never very good at keeping secrets. At first, perhaps, but not later. And when he began to tell me. . .things he couldn't stop. He was like a child— he couldn't sleep with a guilty conscience. He'd come to me straight from their beds. He told me a few years ago what happened the night before the wedding with the. . .striptease girl, and I probably know most of what happened afterwards.'

She lifted her head, refusing to flinch. 'And my pride might have been a little dented at first but I'm not damaged. My self-esteem is intact—he hasn't turned me frigid or bitter. I don't need to be cured or comforted, thank you, James.'

There was a short silence, then he said softly, 'Tessa, you take my breath away.'

She smiled, genuinely now, both with relief at telling someone how it had been and at his astonishment. 'He told me you tried to talk him out of the wedding. Was that why we hardly saw you afterwards?'

'Partly. But we were all busy, all working long hours.' He ran a hand through his hair with vague distraction. 'And then, of course, you came here and there were no other opportunities.' He tilted his head, still obviously having trouble believing she knew everything. 'He really told you that?'

'That you tore him away from her? That you threatened to knock him unconscious so he wouldn't make it to the church?' At his nod she smiled. 'Yes. He was worried you'd say something—you know, when they ask if any-body present knows anything. And he thought you'd lose the ring deliberately, or break his legs, or take me away, or do something else to stop the ceremony.'

'I considered all those things.' James shook his head slowly. 'I thought he would hurt you.' He was frowning now. 'What am I saying? I *knew* that he'd hurt you. I'd thought about saying something for a long time but until the stag night. . .well, until then I thought I might have misjudged him.'

'But you were going to say something at the wedding?'

'I thought I was but when we got to the church you looked so happy. So. . .innocently happy. I couldn't do it. That ceremony was the worst hour of my life.'

'Poor James.' She laughed gently, coming to touch his shoulder to reassure him. 'I was happy. *We* were happy. In a fashion. We were here and I loved that. We were working and I loved that. Everything else I could live with. Richard's not like other people. His upbringing was appalling.'

'That's no excuse.' He captured her hand, holding it there against him and forcing her to acknowledge the warm strength of him. 'The sins of the fathers—'

'Are imitated by the sons,' she finished. 'And perhaps years of therapy might have helped him but I couldn't. As soon as I accepted that, I was all right. Besides, it would have seemed more than a little churlish to fall apart, considering what was going on here in Sadakh. I had an adulterous husband but people here were dying.'

'God, Tessa.' Using the hand at his shoulder, he hugged her closer and buried his face in the side of her neck while his arms encircled her waist—warming her and making her feel protected. 'How do you do it?'

'What?' Disturbed by the sensations he was arousing, she braced her palms against his chest and tilted herself back. 'What do I do?'

'Repeatedly amaze me.'

'I don't know what's so amazing.' Flushed by the heat of him she twisted herself away—unhappily aware of how easy it would be to get used to the sort of intimacy their closeness implied. 'This doesn't change anything,' she said, determined that he understood. 'This is my life now. Here. This hospital. Sadakh. There's no room for anything else. For any *one* else.'

'I don't want to take you away.'

'But you would. Not physically, of course. I wouldn't leave here, but you'd still take part of me. . .part of my energy,' she argued. 'Part of me that I need.'

And she stared at him, willing him to understand although she had no words to describe her certainty that James could touch her where Richard never had. And it was a realisation that scared her.

For years she'd only let herself consider him as a friend, but now she allowed herself to admit that perhaps there had been something more all along, something too disturbing for her to acknowledge consciously.

Being without Richard had never seemed a wrench but she knew with a conviction that frightened her that after being with James, being without him would be unbearable.

She didn't understand it but she knew that she needed him here and she loved him being here and she wanted him to stay. But she couldn't let him get too close.

'You're frightened of me?'

She returned his dark gaze without flinching. 'Yes.'

'I see.' Quietly he moved away. 'I didn't want it to be like that,' he said, and his voice was very quiet and very deep.

For a few days after that life was as normal as she could have expected. She saw less of James than she'd been expecting but, then, they were both busy. When they did meet neither of them mentioned the conversation in her office.

Fazal's jaundice started to fade after his operation and his appetite was returning and Ali, her young patient with leishmaniasis, continued his course of injections and began to eat a little.

Although there were nightly sounds of gunfire far away, and the BBC World Service made a rare mention of Sadakh by reporting heavy troop movements around the capital, they had no emergency admissions.

On Wednesday night Tessa woke to the sounds of shouting and pounding at her door. 'Wake! Wake!' The voice was Mohammed's.

Tessa jumped from her bed, reaching the door in seconds. 'What is it?'

'Casualties.' Mohammed spun back towards the ward block again. 'Rocket and mortar attack in the town. Come now.'

Still in her pyjamas, she raced across. The hospital was a scene of noisy chaos. Helena was triaging the injuries, sending relatives to donate blood, starting intravenous fluids and antibiotics and giving tetanus shots to casualties as they arrived.

James, already up and dressed in theatre blues, ran

past her. He was carrying a child soaked with blood while a weeping man ran alongside them, his bloody hand under the child's arm trying to stem the flow of blood. 'Ruptured axillary artery,' James called to her. 'I'll be in Theatre.'

Helena looked up from a new admission. 'Tessa, abdominal trauma. You'd better take him now—I don't think he can wait for James.' She directed two attendants to follow her with their casualty.

There were two theatres, joined by a common scrub and anaesthetic area, and as normal when they had a lot of work and there would be no time for cleaning between operations they worked relatively clean procedures in one room, and dirty in the second. Tessa took her patient to the second theatre.

He was unconscious, his abdomen bloody with wounds and rigidly stiff where it was still intact. The most likely diagnosis was a perforated bowel from mortar fragments, but when she opened she found his spleen severely torn, the lower pole almost mush.

'I'll have to take the spleen,' she told Axel, who was moving between the theatres, supervising each of the nurses' anaesthetics. 'Plus resection and oversewing of perforated small bowel.'

'OK.' He hooked up a bag of blood. 'Want James?'

'Ask him to look in when he can,' she confirmed, beginning to clamp the blood vessels around the stomach. She'd performed this sort of procedure before in emergencies but she'd welcome his advice. 'He'll need as much blood as you can get—he's lost a lot.'

James came as she was beginning on the bowel. Freshly scrubbed, he bent over and inspected her work, keeping his hands away so he wouldn't need to scrub again for his own case. 'Good job. Well done.'

The doors opened and another trolley was wheeled behind her into the theatre. James said, 'There's another abdomen to start. Can you manage here?'

'Yes.' She didn't lift her eyes from her work. Speed

was as important as accuracy at times like this. 'How's the child?'

'She's kept the arm.'

'Many more?'

'About another dozen.' He walked to the other bed. 'Mostly limb injuries.' Tessa heard him saying something to Monique who was scrubbing for him since she was the only nurse, apart from Helena, who spoke English. 'Ready, Axel?'

'Go, James.'

Tessa's patient was stable when she finished. Still pale, he'd only had four units of blood—the most they could spare and less than he'd lost—but he was young and looked fit and Axel was confident he'd manage with that.

Leaving him to the nurses who were covering Recovery, Tessa pulled off her gloves and scrubbed again.

Her next patient was waiting in the other theatre. Another young man, this time with mortar-shell trauma to his left leg. Large fragments had pierced his thigh, crushing and damaging the surrounding tissues, although the bone itself—apart from a few tiny splintered fragments—had not fractured.

Tessa checked that his foot pulses were intact, which they were, meaning that the blood supply hadn't been compromised. After applying antiseptic to the wounds, she cut away the pulped areas of skin which had been destroyed by the projectiles along with an extra strip of skin around the circumference of the main wound.

'It's messy,' she told Axel when he briefly returned. 'Loads of shell fragments.' Systematically she tracked the metal pieces, opening the paths they'd made through the tissues, cleaning and removing dead and dying tissue as she went.

To complete, she doused the wounds with cleansing hydrogen peroxide.

After waiting a few minutes to be sure that all the bleeding had stopped she left the wound unsutured and open, covering it with an absorbent, fluffy gauze which would let any discharge that needed to escape seep through and holding the dressing in place with broad, loose-fitting bandages.

Pushing herself away from the table, she went and scrubbed again for the next case—another debridement like the last, this time of the left leg and arm.

Her fourth case, a middle-aged man, also had shell damage, but this time the fragments had smashed his knee and exited behind it, severing his artery so that when she released the tourniquet—which one of their paramedics must have applied—blood poured out of the wound, while his lower leg and foot remained cold and pulseless. She probed the area and above it but couldn't find either the artery to control it or a pulse.

He was losing blood and she needed help. 'James?'

He was working at the other table and came immediately. Khan, who was scrubbing for Tessa, pulled a second pair of gloves over the ones James was wearing and James inspected the wound, feeling the area she'd explored.

He easily found and clamped off a section of tissue enclosing the artery she hadn't managed to locate. He tightened the tourniquet again. 'You'll have to amputate,' he said flatly, drawing a line along the skin above her patient's knee to show her the level she should go for. 'You've no choice—it's irreparable here. All right?'

'Yes.' She smiled her thanks behind her mask. If she was tired then he must be doubly so—he was doing two patients to her one, but the vivid energy of his gaze belied it. 'Thanks.'

'That's what I'm here for,' he said quietly, returning to his patient. 'Leave it open. We'll close in a few days once we see how it's going. OK?'

'OK.' Tessa took the scalpel Khan offered her and began to cut.

*   *   *

They finished operating about midday. Then she and Axel and Mohammed and James went around all their new admissions together, discussing each case and formulating management plans.

They'd had twenty-two admissions overnight and had operated on eighteen, all of whom were still alive. The other four admissions had been two children with minor limb injuries which had not required surgery and two adult men with closed fractures which Mohammed had reduced and plastered under local anaesthetic.

Mohammed told them that twelve people had died in the attack and that more trouble was expected.

'We have to have more blood.' Tessa directed her comments to Mohammed, who was best equipped to muster the technicians and take charge of finding it. 'Every person who walks into this building should be asked to donate.'

James said, 'I'm O negative. I'm happy to give.'

'Thanks.' Mohammed had already given blood. Axel's group was unhelpful here, but Tessa had the same blood group as James—the type that could be donated to almost anyone—and she told him she'd go with him after the round to give.

Axel and Mohammed left when they finished seeing the acute admissions and she and James worked through the wards systematically, discharging all the patients they could to clear beds.

Ali, her patient with leishmaniasis, was due for his sixth dose of intravenous therapy. It was too soon for any dramatic improvement in his condition but his appetite had recovered and Tessa decided that he could continue his treatment as an outpatient. She arranged for him to attend daily for the rest of his course, stressing how important it was that he completed the treatment.

Fazal's jaundice, five days post-surgery, was fading fast. He was hungry and had managed breakfast. James inspected his wound and his abdomen, pronouncing the beaming man fit and well. 'Home in a few days once we take the sutures out,' he declared. 'His village is too far away to expect him to come back just for that.'

After they'd finished the round Tessa took James to the laboratory. 'We'll have to do each other,' she said, fishing out two blood bags and their attached large needles. 'Mohammed and the technicians must be away doing other volunteers.'

There was no bed in the room and James sat on a stool and rolled up his sleeve, eyeing the advancing needle warily. 'Are you going to use local with that?'

She avoided his eyes. 'Of course.' She left the half-sheathed needle on the bench, swabbed his arm with iodine solution and twisted her tourniquet around his muscled upper arm, waiting a few seconds for his skin to dry and for the vessels to fill. 'Nice veins.'

'Hmm.' He was watching her—she could feel it. 'Where's the anaesthetic?'

'Coming.' She turned so he couldn't see her, unsheathed the blood needle and then swung back, swiftly inserting it into a large vein before he had a chance to complain.

'How did I know that was going to happen?' he said dryly, and she realised he hadn't even flinched as the needle pierced his skin.

She waited until the red fluid began drizzling into the plastic bag then lowered the bag to the floor. 'I'm sorry. I know that's unethical but we don't have enough anaesthetic to waste any on ourselves, and last time I did this without using any Richard went crazy. It doesn't hurt much so today I thought I'd try surprise tactics.'

'That's all right.' He eyed her appraisingly. 'You next.'

'Yes.' She hopped up onto a stool beside him, unworried. James did everything well—he wouldn't hurt her. 'Pump your fist.'

The movement made the muscles in his forearm work and she averted her eyes. 'I should have asked a few things before this,' she told him, resting her elbow on the bench and leaning her head to study him assessingly.

'History of hepatitis? HIV? IV drug use? Male sexual partners?'

'No. No. No. Never.'

'Aspirin? Unexplained weight loss? Night sweats?'

'No. No.' Then he looked at her meaningfully. 'Yes, lately.'

'Yes, lately?'

He frowned, then said slowly, 'Not medically significant. Forget it.'

Tessa frowned. Was he unwell? 'Not medically significant?'

James's eyes darkened. 'You don't want to know.'

'Yes, I do.' Alarmed now, she sat up straight. All sorts of diseases caused night sweats and many of them were sinister. She'd heard there'd been increasing numbers of tuberculosis admissions to London hospitals. What if he'd developed it? Or something worse? She couldn't treat him properly here. He'd have to go back to Britain. She'd lose him. 'Do you or do you not wake up hot and sweating during the night?'

'Tessa,' he said tightly, 'you are sleeping less than a foot away from me, through a wall which could easily be paper. You know what I want. What the hell do you expect?'

CHAPTER SEVEN

'Oh.' In her relief, Tessa laughed. 'You mean me? Oh. I never thought... I don't know what to say.' James looked irritated and that increased her amusement. 'Nobody's ever said anything like that to me before. I think... I think... Should I be flattered?' She laughed again. 'Oh, James, sorry. I could move you. Helena sleeps with Axel so her room, next to Monique's, is normally free.'

'I'll stay where I am,' he growled.

'But Monique won't mind—'

'Shut up.'

'But, then, it would be the same problem,' she said, sobering. 'Only with Monique.'

James's eyes narrowed. Somehow keeping his blood-donor arm straight, he used his free arm to haul her from her stool and closer to him so that she half stood, half sat, between his legs with her hands on his shoulders. 'I suppose I can blame Richard for this,' he muttered darkly. 'Tessa, forget Monique. The woman does nothing for me. Frankly, she could walk in here naked and I wouldn't notice. OK?'

'Yes.' She'd tensed at the mention of Richard but then realised that James couldn't have understood the significance of his words. Unable to stop herself, she hugged him and squeezed him close, joy warming her as much as he was, although she knew she had no right to be so happy.

'You, however, are different.' He disentangled her arms and put her away from him, his mouth set tight. 'Even with all your clothes on. Unless you're telling me you've changed your mind?'

'No.' Guiltily aware that her gesture had been seen as

provocative, she drew further away, flushing. 'I'm sorry. You're nice to hug. This is going to be difficult, isn't it?'

'More so for me, I suspect.' His smile was wry but strained. 'There's a full unit there,' he said, drawing her attention to the bulging bag. 'Do you just want one?'

'For now.' Her smile felt stiff. 'Perhaps in a few days we'll take another.'

She snapped off the tourniquet and slid the needle out, pressing a square of gauze to his arm for him to hold while she knotted the tubing and cut free the needle. Then she labelled the bag, adding a note of explanation so that their technician understood to test it.

She prepared a bag for herself, gave it to James and sat on her stool, a lingering self-consciousness making her movements a little stiff as she rolled up her sleeve. 'My veins aren't as good,' she apologised when he tightened the tourniquet around her arm. 'Usually they have trouble finding them.'

'They're good enough.' Cool fingers probed the soft skin of the inside of her elbow, raising goose bumps on her arms. He swabbed her with iodine and said quietly, 'Ready?'

'Yes.'

She watched him insert the needle and there was no pain, merely a smooth, cold feeling as it slid into her vein. He taped it to hold it in place, then loosened the tourniquet slightly and let the bag fall to the floor where the blood began to pool inside it.

He leaned back against the bench and folded his arms. 'How often do you give?'

'When it's needed.' She watched her blood flowing through the transparent tubing. 'I last gave a unit two weeks ago. Technically, I know that's too often but I'm not anaemic—I can afford to be generous.'

'Two weeks is far too often.' He was frowning.

'It's necessary.' She met his questioning gaze calmly. 'We had a seventeen-year-old girl with a rare blood group and a severe haemorrhage after her first baby was born.

She would have died without blood, and we didn't have enough. There wasn't any choice.'

'You could have waited this time.'

Seeing that he was eyeing the needle as if tempted to haul it out, she slapped her hand over it. 'We'll need this,' she said. 'If not tonight then tomorrow. If not tomorrow then soon after.'

'Take more of mine.'

'I will.' She smiled, relaxing. 'Of course I will. When we need it. You don't have to ask twice.'

'And how do you know you're not anaemic?' He turned her free hand over and studied it, then gently exposed her lower eyelid, obviously checking her colouring. 'You're pale.'

'I'm disgustingly healthy,' she countered, showing him her teeth so he could see how pink her gums were. 'I haven't had a day sick in five years.'

'Hmm.'

But he didn't look convinced, and she wondered at the novelty of having someone concerned about her when she was so used to being the one who did the worrying about other people. 'I can look after myself,' she chided. 'I've been doing it for years.'

'That doesn't mean you've been doing it well,' he argued. 'You give too much of yourself.'

'There's no alternative here.'

'That doesn't make it good.'

'It's what I want.' And she smiled at the frustration he made no effort to conceal. 'It's my life, James. I appreciate your concern but there's no point in trying to change anything—I won't let you.'

He returned her smile slowly. 'You're a stubborn woman, Tessa Mathesson.'

'Yes.' She wasn't ashamed of that. She pumped her fist then leaned forward a little and looked down at the bag. 'Full, I think.'

He withdrew the needle and gave her gauze to hold against the puncture to stem the bleeding. 'Do I tie this?'

'Yes.' She nodded as he copied the knot she'd done earlier. 'The needle goes in the covered box over there.' She stood to show him, hovered and suddenly sat back on her stool when her head spun.

'Tessa. . .?' James growled, having caught her expression.

'I'm fine.' She lowered her head between her legs and took three deep breaths. Perhaps he'd been right about twice in two weeks being too heavy a donation—especially considering that she'd given another unit only a few weeks before that.

But, even if his doubts had been warranted, she wasn't going to admit it to him. Slowly she lifted her head, relieved when all was steady. 'I'm fine,' she repeated, defensively now. She'd just have to be a little careful.

'Stay there.' He held up the bulging bag. 'I'll give you this back.'

'No.' She stood very slowly, squeezing the muscles in her calves. All was fine. 'Don't be ridiculous. Someone will need it more than I do.' She yawned. 'I'll check the wards again before I go to Outpatients. There's no clinic today but people with minor injuries from last night may just turn up.'

They'd have missed lunch but there would be food left in the kitchen and she'd grab something. 'Why don't you eat then get some rest?' she suggested, taking the blood slowly to the fridge. 'It might be busy again tonight.'

'*I'll* check the wards.' James was looking at her hard. 'And then I'll come to clinic. Tessa, are you all right?'

'Stop fussing.' She opened the door, waiting for him to follow her out. 'I'll go to Children's, then, but it'd be great if you could just look in on the rest. Thanks.'

Some patients, as she'd suspected, did come to clinic, with injuries secondary to the attack the night before. No one required admission, merely tetanus shots and cleansing and dressing of their wounds.

Afterwards she and James and Mohammed took tea

together in the mess; the others were trying to get some sleep.

Mohammed had had a productive afternoon, building up their blood supplies and helping the technicians sterilise all the surgical equipment they'd used the night before so everything was ready for use again.

'Tessa, I have been watching you a little this afternoon,' Mohammed said, as she went to fetch them a second cup of the tea she'd prepared. 'And for the first time in many years you are walking slowly,' he added approvingly. 'Very good. I think you are learning from me.'

'She hasn't learned anything.' James scowled. 'She's only got two red blood cells left. If she moves quickly she'll fall over.'

'Stop exaggerating.' She passed Mohammed his cup. 'Take no notice, Mohammed. James has decided to become my mother.'

'You need a mother.' James took the tea she offered him, watching her broodingly. 'Do you have one?'

'Yes.' She blinked, surprised by the question. Surely he'd met at least some of her family at the wedding? 'In fact, I have two.'

But James's expression suggested that he either hadn't met any of her relatives or didn't remember, and she recalled that he'd seemed preoccupied at the ceremony and had left the reception early.

'Two?' he asked.

'My parents divorced when I was very young,' she told him, 'and both remarried. I have two of each, plus six stepsisters and five stepbrothers. The oldest is twenty-six, the youngest seven and there are two sets of twins. Do you want to see my photos?'

'Not right now.' He looked taken aback, and she remembered that he was an only child. Probably horrified at the thought of her family, she realised.

'No wonder there's this craving of yours for open spaces,' he said shrewdly.

She laughed, conceding that he had a point. 'They might be part of the reason I find Sadakh so appealing,' she admitted. 'As a teenager, I had to share a room with three of my sisters. I love them all, of course, but they're a little overwhelming *en masse*.'

'What do they all think of you working out here?'

'Is that important?'

'Does that mean they disapprove?'

His expression suggested that they should and Tessa smiled. 'They don't make judgements like that,' she said lightly.

As the oldest of such a large brood her parents seemed now more like friends to her than guardians. They had reservations, of course, about her living in Sadakh— she sensed that—but they led busy lives and had eight grandchildren to distract them from worrying about her. And they knew her well enough to know she made up her own mind on the things that were important to her. 'At least, they don't make judgements like that out loud,' she added, returning to his question about whether her parents disapproved of her work.

'They would be wasting their time.' Mohammed was beaming, clearly enjoying their conversation. 'Tessa would not listen.'

'That's right.' She laughed with him. 'Mohammed, you know me too well.'

'It has been a long time.' He beamed at James. 'Only when it comes to work does the kitten become a tiger,' he announced. 'Watch and you will see her.'

'It isn't just her work,' said James, regarding Tessa with a gentle, knowing amusement which made her flush.

The first sounds of the early evening call to prayer began drifting from the town and Mohammed bent, drawing her gaze. He collected his prayer mat. 'I am going to my prayers and then I will sleep.'

'Helena's old room is spare,' she told him. When Mohammed's family was away he normally slept in a hammock near the hospital entrance but it was early and he wouldn't get much rest while there were still people about. 'You're welcome to it if you want to stay here.'

'I shall see. Thank you.' He bowed his head slightly in farewell and left them.

Ignoring James's I-told-you-so expression as he registered the wary way she was moving, Tessa stood too—very carefully, for she was still finding herself prone to light-headedness. 'I think I'll rest before dinner,' she said, collecting their mugs. 'Do you want more tea?'

'Never in my life,' he said, although she'd just seen him drink two full cups. 'I've never tasted anything so foul. Did Richard leave any Scotch behind?'

'Cordial bottle in the newspaper cupboard,' she confirmed, her frown clearing as she realised that James would never be irresponsible enough to drink himself into a state which would prevent him from operating. 'See you at dinner.'

But instead she slept through the night until five next morning when hunger drove her from bed. She ate several spoonfuls of peanut butter, before serving herself some of the rice mixed with grated carrots and pine nuts that she found left for her in the kitchen.

As she scraped the plate clean she heard a noise, looked up and saw James there, watching her. She noted his theatre blues with a frown. 'You've been working?'

'Bullet wound from yesterday,' he confirmed quietly. 'Straight through his flank. God knows how it missed his kidney but it did.'

'Not brought in until now?'

'Brought in around two. I've just finished him. I don't think it had anything to do with the bomb,' he told her, coming to light the gas for water. 'I couldn't understand much of his history, of course, but Mohammed said something about a family feud.'

'Oh.' She pushed her empty plate away. 'Someone should have called me. Who scrubbed?'

'Helena. And it was a surgical case—that's my job.

There was no reason to call you.' He frowned at her. 'Still dizzy?'

'No.' She wasn't going to admit anything. 'Any other problems?'

'All quiet.' The water had boiled and he poured it into the teapot. 'Love the pyjamas.'

She tucked the flannelette top firmly under her bottom. Not used to giving her clothing a second thought, she suddenly found herself wishing she'd worn the trousers as well. Telling herself that was just because the early morning was chilly—and not because she was self-conscious about James seeing her—she said, 'Marks and Spencer's.' When Richard had left them behind she'd seen no point in not making use of them.

James's eyes twinkled mockingly when he passed her tea and she knew he'd noted the way she'd swivelled her bare legs under the table. 'Relax, Tessa. I'm not about to jump on you. It's far too early in the morning.'

She flushed. 'How's Nazif?' she asked, referring to the man she'd performed the splenectomy on. He'd had a slight temperature the previous day and she'd been worrying about him.

'Afebrile and asleep,' he drawled, taking the seat opposite her. 'Did you sleep well?'

'Wonderfully.' She was flustered now. 'You?'

'Not especially.' He watched her over the rim of his drink as he took a few long swallows. 'I need some language lessons—want to be my teacher?'

'You're only here a few months.' She tilted her head. 'Do you really need lessons?'

'If I'm to work with any nurse but Monique or Helena,' he answered. 'And they're going to be needed in other places.'

'Mohammed taught me. I could ask—'

'He suggested you,' he said smoothly.

'I bet he did.' Mohammed had taken a shine to James and Tessa suspected she was right to be suspicious of his motives but they were all busy and it wasn't fair to ask any of the others.

Besides, James's need was genuine—she could hardly allow her vow to keep more distance between them to interfere with his ability to work. 'I'd be happy to,' she said finally. 'Do you know any other languages?'

'School French and Latin.' He smiled. 'Shall we aim for an hour a day?'

'We can try. Half an hour's probably more realistic at the moment.'

'Fine.'

'Evenings would be best.' Tessa pushed her chair back, deciding she was foolish to be embarrassed about what she was wearing. It wasn't as if he hadn't seen a pair of legs before, and hers were the same as everyone else's. 'Say, around nine?'

'I'm looking forward to it already.'

She looked at him sharply but there was nothing calculating in the eyes that met hers—only amusement. The eyes dropped to her legs and she stood there, waiting, silently daring him to say something. His gaze rose to meet hers again, only his was warm and gentle, as if he understood her sudden shyness. She didn't know what to say and so she ran away.

In the early part of the afternoon, once she'd finished on the wards, she went to her office to work out her next supply order. One shipment was two days overdue but already she needed to prepare for the next. As it was the Holy Day there was no outpatient session scheduled and she had spare time.

Over dinner, another of Axel's curry delights, James made a remark about how peaceful it was that evening.

'Friday,' Helena explained. 'It's usually quiet.'

'When the Russians were here the fighting was worst on Fridays,' Tessa added. 'Part of their tactics.'

'Which failed,' Axel said triumphantly, as if the news of the Russian defeat was fresh.

'I'm sick of always talking about this war,' Monique

said irritably. She rested her fork on the edge of her plate, then pushed it away. 'I am bored. James. I would like a walk but it is not safe alone. Will you come with me?'

'Sorry. I'm having a language lesson.' He looked at Tessa. 'Tessa's teaching me.'

'I decided we'd best start tomorrow,' Tessa said, suddenly cold. 'I need to prepare.'

His eyes held hers for one long moment and whatever he saw in hers made his harden. 'A walk, then,' he said, rising. 'Anyone else interested?'

But nobody else was, and the young nurse's flushed face and triumphant eyes betrayed her excitement.

After they'd left the room was extraordinarily still. Tessa stood abruptly and collected the still half-laden plates. 'Anyone for tea?' she said brightly.

Helena followed her to the kitchen. 'Monique is a foolish child,' she said bluntly. 'And you are an adult but you are even stupider.'

Tessa concentrated on filling the kettle. 'He could have said no.'

'He couldn't. She told him it was dangerous for her to walk alone.' The Dutch nurse snorted. 'Dangerous? Ha! Dangerous for him, perhaps, alone with her.'

'He makes his own decisions.'

'What's wrong with you? Are you testing him?'

'I don't know what you're talking about.' Tessa stared at the kettle. 'There's no test.'

'James is not Richard,' Helena said, sounding as if she was fuming.

'I know,' she retorted, tired—totally tired of that refrain. 'I know he's not Richard.'

'Then you know he is not about to sleep with that girl.'

Tessa's head snapped up at that. 'Who told you?' she demanded hoarsely.

Helena threw her arms into the air. 'We all know. Of course we know. Until just now I thought it was you who didn't realise, but when I saw your face as James left with her I understood. Monique made sure we knew about Richard. That is her way. Her proof of her woman-hood, if you like. Don't you understand her at all?'

'Richard was to blame,' Tessa said tightly. 'She was young and impressionable; she'd only just arrived. He took advantage—'

'Richard and Monique, they are the same sort of people,' Helena insisted. 'He took no advantage. You're so naïve about some things, Tessa. You see only the good in people. You make excuses for bad behaviour where there is no excuse. Wake up before it is too late. We are all good and bad mixed, all of us. Monique is a good nurse, but that does not mean she is not also spoilt and manipulative.'

'James can take care of himself.'

'Of course he can.' Helena took the kettle from her when it seemed about to spill. 'But he is a man and they are different to us. Even the best ones. If you continue to push him towards her he might decide you truly don't want him.'

'But I don't.'

'Ha!' Helena slammed the mugs on to the bench, then poured the tea. 'You two, you watch each other all the time—even I have noticed this. And you are not a nun, Tessa, no matter how you pretend. A man like James will be good for you. *Sex* will be good for you.'

Tessa stared at her, startled, but Helena didn't appear to expect her to say anything because she promptly stacked three mugs of tea onto a tray and headed for the door.

Tessa took the remaining tea and walked quickly across to her office, careful not to look around in case she spotted James and Monique locked in some torrid embrace in the distance. That would make everything he'd said to her the day before in the laboratory untrue, and she didn't want to know that. 'I'm not testing him,' she told herself, knowing that subconsciously she probably was.

'And I'm not jealous.' Only she definitely was, and it

was an emotion she wasn't used to. Richard's exploits hadn't made her jealous, merely resigned. Everything was different with James.

The following morning, unusually for Monique, she was up when Tessa walked in for breakfast. Monique *and* James. James's hooded eyes met hers briefly yet speakingly, but Monique greeted her with lively chirpiness.

Tessa managed a small smile, telling herself that she should be pleased, at least, that someone was enjoying this.

'I slept wonderfully,' Monique crowed, stretching her arms above her head. 'It was a beautiful sunrise.'

'Wasn't it?' Busying herself spreading toast with peanut butter, Tessa couldn't quite stop her eyebrows rising. The sunrise between the mountains had been as beautiful as always but, then, she supposed, annoyed with herself for her churlishness, Monique didn't often rise that early. 'Monique, are you helping on the wards this morning?'

'Oh, I thought I'd scrub for James,' she replied airily. 'I will speak with Helena. I am sure she will not mind giving up the session.' And then she touched James's forearm, drawing what Tessa saw was a mildly weary look from him. 'We are so good together,' she gushed. 'You and I. I understand your needs before you do.'

'That's handy.' Tessa met James's dark look with careful calm, suddenly cross with herself for ever doubting that she could trust him.

James had told her the truth when he'd said he had no interest in Monique. And, despite the nurse's rather touching efforts to stamp her possessiveness on him, it was clear he remained unimpressed.

Despite the pleasure that gave her, pleasure she wasn't entitled to, she felt a brief pang of worry for Monique. Helena's comments last night had cynically ignored Monique's youth and vulnerability, attributes that concerned Tessa. Monique had been terribly hurt by Richard's abrupt departure from Sadakh, whereas she, his wife, had merely been relieved that he'd left with so little fuss.

And the small worries she had had about Richard's departure had been minimised by Jean-Paul's confident assurance that he could cope with the increased surgical load he would inherit.

But she didn't want to see Monique hurt again; didn't want to have to comfort her again through those hours and hours of dreadful weeping which Helena and Axel had somehow managed to ignore but which she hadn't been able to.

It was another reason, even if she didn't need one, not to become involved with James herself.

She ate her toast quickly and left them, taking her tea to her office, but James must have followed her because he pushed open the door only seconds after she'd sat at her desk.

'I want to see the wards before Theatre,' he said quietly. 'Come and translate?'

'Of course.' She left her tea and went with him.

Fazal had eaten a good breakfast. His jaundice was faint and his wound was clean and healthy. 'Sutures out today,' James said, and Tessa translated for the nurse who was with them. 'Eat and home.' He looked at Tessa. 'How about follow-up here?'

'Not routine,' she explained. 'Otherwise we'd be swamped.'

'No follow-up, then. Return SOS. OK?'

'Fine.' She explained that to Fazal and he nodded solemn thanks, clasping James's hand briefly in appreciation.

Nazif, the man she'd performed the splenectomy and bowel repair on, had begun to take sips of liquid, his temperature was normal this morning and his abdomen was as soft as could be expected.

'We'll operate again tomorrow and close the wounds,' James said approvingly 'I'll leave the dressings until then.' He checked under Nazif's eyes. 'Haemoglobin?'

'Ten,' the nurse said, smiling proudly at this small command of English.

'Thank you.' James grinned at him. 'You've been holding out on me.'

But that was beyond the nurse's limits. Tessa translated James's words and was rewarded with another beam.

'English. Yes,' he said happily, adding in his own language, 'I will learn every day.'

They checked each of their emergency admissions from Wednesday night. Of the men, all but one of the ones who'd undergone a limb amputation or wound debridement had normal temperatures and were otherwise all right. The gauze strips beneath the bandages were clean so they didn't disturb anything, leaving the dressings until later in the week when they'd inspect and probably close the wounds under anaesthetic.

'Four to six days' delay's my preference,' James said, confirming the timing Tessa herself used.

The delay between initial surgery and closing the wounds reduced the risk of infections such as gangrene and was almost a universal protocol with the traumatic wounds they encountered, except in cases such as joint or hand wounds when it was more important to cover the delicate tissues which had been exposed, or facial wounds where the tissues seemed to heal well and cleanly regardless.

The last patient, though, a young man who'd had a large thigh wound debrided by Mohammed, was feverish this morning. His face and neck were flushed and hot and his leg, above the bandages, was swollen.

'No cough, no pain, no urinary symptoms,' Tessa said, translating his words into English for James.

'Here's the problem.' James released the bandages, revealing a green-tinged staining of the gauze which covered their patient's wound and, thankfully, only a faint skin pressure mark from where the bandage must have been tight for only a short time.

'Theatre this morning,' he declared, not touching the

dressings which were adhering to the wound. 'Did he have anti-tetanus and antibiotics?'

Tessa checked the chart. 'Yes, to both. Still on penicillin.'

'Breakfast?'

'Some rice.' She checked with the nurse. 'When?'

'Two hours ago.'

'We'll put him third on the list, then,' said James, when she'd translated. 'He'll need more penicillin and a loading dose of gentamicin in the meantime.'

While he went to fetch the drugs Tessa explained to the patient—and to his wife and his sisters who sat with him and had been with him almost continually since his admission—that there was infection in the wound and they had to operate again.

'So be it.' He was stoical, but his sisters began to weep, sobbing loudly through their veils.

Tessa tried to explain that the procedure would be straightforward but the women were inconsolable. Then she remembered that his mother had died in the attack.

Hardly surprising, she thought sadly, that their emotions were still in turmoil. 'God will be with him,' she said simply, quickly explaining the reason for their grief to James who'd returned with the antibiotics and was obviously startled by the women's reactions.

After administering the drugs, they went to the children's ward. The young girl whose axillary artery had been torn was up and about, using her good arm to help feed some of the younger children. Her mother wasn't there this morning and she smiled shyly at them as they approached, returning to her bed at Tessa's gentle request.

Her arm was still splinted and bandaged but her wrist was exposed and the colour in her hand was normal.

James examined her wrist pulses and nodded approvingly. 'Full.' He tested nerve function in her hand by asking her to squeeze his finger, then to spread her fingers while he tried to close them and finally to grip a sheet of Tessa's notepaper between her fingers while he tried to pull it away.

'Looks like she's going to have full function,' Tessa said, relieved she hadn't had to operate on the child herself. In an emergency, of course, she'd have tackled the repair, but she recognised she probably wouldn't have been able to save the girl's arm. 'Lucky you were here.'

'Don't underestimate yourself,' he said quietly. 'The work I've seen you doing is impressive.'

'I get by,' she countered. 'Just.' While James's work was inspiring.

After seeing the surgical cases, he went to Theatre, and when she'd finished with the rest of her patients she followed him, curious about the infected leg wound they'd seen earlier.

At James's suggestion she scrubbed, joining him as he lifted free the gauze which had hardened into a cast except for the area where the discharge had dampened it.

'It's not gangrene,' he said quietly, giving her a small retractor to hold back the edges of the wound so he could swab away the discharge. 'No smell.'

Tessa raised the retractor to give him better access as he irrigated the area with saline. Gas gangrene was a not unknown complication of this sort of injury, but with good initial wound surgery and antibiotic treatment they rarely saw it unless the injury was days old before it reached them. 'Much dead tissue?'

'Not a lot.' Using the scalpel Monique passed him, James cleared away the debris at the surface then excised a small section of pale muscle. 'Mohammed did a good job.'

He put down the scalpel and probed, first with forceps and then with his finger, finally withdrawing a small fragment of metal and dislodging a large collection of inflammatory fluid and pus.

'Shrapnel,' he said calmly, dropping the fragment into one of Monique's bowls. 'Obviously too deep to feel at first wound surgery. The infection built up behind it.'

Tessa relaxed. 'All right, otherwise?'

'He's going to be fine.' James removed a large blood clot from the base of the wound and she buzzed a couple of small vessels that had started to bleed.

'We'll leave it open again,' James said, swabbing now with hydrogen peroxide. 'Inspect with a view to closing in four days.' He stood back and walked around behind Monique to the foot of the trolley and Tessa gently pressed dressing gauze into the wound.

James raised their patient's foot so she could bandage his thigh. 'Going to stay?' he asked.

'For the skin graft?' she said.

'You can do it,' he said easily. 'I'll supervise.'

Although she heard Monique click her tongue irritably, it was too good an offer for Tessa to refuse. James wouldn't be here indefinitely, and she had to take teaching whenever she could get it.

The graft only took about thirty minutes and was a straightforward procedure where she shaved a thin spread of skin from one thigh and used it to cover a defect left by a bullet in the other.

'You're a good teacher,' she told him as they washed their hands afterwards, smiling as she imagined how hard the junior doctors at his own hospital must fight to get onto his rotation. 'And I get you for free.'

'Not free, Tessa.' He still wore his mask and above it his eyes laughed at her. 'I haven't sent you my bill yet.'

'Don't hurry.' She smiled. 'If I thought about the income you must be sacrificing while you're here I'd have nightmares. Rest assured, your bill would bankrupt me.'

'From what I've seen, it'd probably bankrupt Sadakh,' he said easily, not sounding especially concerned. 'Unless there's oil here.'

'There might be.' She dried her hands on the towel he passed her. 'There's certainly coal and gas and uranium. But everyone's too busy fighting to exploit them.'

'They haven't been fighting today. It's been quiet.'

'It stops and starts like this.' She untied her mask, threw it into the laundry basket and followed him into the changing room. They didn't have separate facilities for males and females but there was a shoulder-high carved wooden screen which the women conventionally used and Tessa walked behind that.

'After clinic I want to go into town to see Ahmad again,' she said, her back to him as she hauled her theatre smock over her head. She hurled it towards a laundry bin. 'Remember the child with the mysterious fever you saw on your first day?' She tugged off her pants, reached for the jeans she'd discarded earlier and pulled them on, wiggling them over her hips before she zipped them up. 'I just want to check he's still OK. If there's a problem from the surgery there should definitely be signs by now.'

She looked around for her top. She'd been in a hurry when she'd been changing so she could have flung it anywhere. 'You're welcome to come with me, if you want. Mohammed's busy today so he'll be pleased if you could drive me.' When he didn't reply she turned around. 'James. . .?'

And then her mouth dried. Her arms came up, crossing onto each shoulder and shielding her breasts.

Still in theatre blues, he hadn't moved from where he'd been standing when they'd first walked into the room. But as he was so much taller than the other men who used the room he could easily see over the barrier. And he wasn't looking away.

CHAPTER EIGHT

'FINISH dressing, Tessa.'

She couldn't move; James held her mesmerised. 'You shouldn't be looking—'

'Don't think about what I should or shouldn't be doing. Just dress.'

Blushing from her bare toes to her ruffled hair, she turned away from him again, found her shirt and buttoned it to her neck with trembling fingers. 'This is ridiculous,' she said shakily, turning back to meet his brooding regard when she was covered again. 'You're a doctor. You've seen hundreds of naked women.'

'It isn't the same.'

'Why didn't you tell me you could see?'

'You are joking, aren't you?' He folded his arms, still watching her.

'It wasn't polite.'

'That's the least of your problems,' he said darkly. 'Are you coming out from there?'

'I don't know.' She stuffed her feet back into the clogs she'd been wearing, then mustered a self-conscious smile. 'I feel like a teenager.'

'Good.'

She walked around the screen and said softly, 'James, this has to stop. It's crazy.'

'Isn't it?' He moved, catching her arm and swinging her towards him, slowly, as if he was waiting for her to stop him—only she couldn't. Despite her words, she couldn't do anything but go to him.

Calmly, deliberately, his hand lifted to her waist, and he held it there and she could feel the warmth of him through the cotton of her shirt. Then, his eyes holding hers, he moved his hand and cupped one small, tight breast.

Tessa gasped. Fabric protected her flesh from his touch but still she burned. Her eyes clung to the darkness of his. 'Helena tells me I need sex,' she whispered.

'Helena's a sensible woman.' James's mouth lowered. 'But, then, I'm biased.'

She turned her head so that his mouth missed hers and brushed her cheek, then her chin and her throat.

'You told me you didn't want to frighten me.'

'You don't have to be frightened.' He put her slightly away from him and she saw him watch the way his hand moved slowly back and forth across her right breast, scrunching the cotton. He stared at his hand as if the movement fascinated him. 'I don't want to hurt you.' His thumb stroked her nipple through the fabric. 'Just touch you.'

She looked down, barely able to breathe, and shivered as both her nipples, their peaks outlined beneath her shirt, quivered in arousal. 'Like this?'

'More than this.' His hand stopped, cupped her, held her. 'Much, much more than this.'

She swallowed, then slowly allowed herself to look up again to meet the vividly demanding look in his eyes. 'James, please don't—'

At that moment the door from Theatres swung open a little, hitting James's back, and she heard Monique's voice saying something and James was holding the door while Tessa moved away from him and wiped her flushed face and smoothed her hair. Then she saw Monique, staring at her as if amazed that she was still there. Tessa realised that it was very late and she muttered something silly and hurried away, ignoring James's urgent command that she stopped, for she was late for clinic and people would be waiting to see her.

Helena took one look at her face and shooed her into a side-room. 'You work in there,' she said firmly. 'I will translate for James when he arrives, and Axel and Monique can get by on their own.'

'I'm all right,' she said, not understanding Helena's concern.

'It is not every day that you spend thirty minutes shut away with a man like James,' countered the nurse lightly, proving that nothing went unnoticed. 'Unfortunately,' she added, scooting away.

Tessa groaned. She lowered her head to her hands, squeezed her eyes shut and made a determined attempt to wipe the past half-hour from her mind.

James came to see her after the clinic. 'Ready for town?' he said calmly, walking carelessly into the room as if nothing untoward had happened.

Tessa blinked at him. 'Town?'

'Ahmad. You asked me to drive you. Have you forgotten?'

'I didn't realise you were listening.'

'Admittedly, I was preoccupied,' he said softly, 'but not deaf.'

She flushed, covering her confusion by gathering together the notes on the children she'd just seen. 'OK,' she said. 'Fine. Thank you. I'd appreciate a lift.' She left the notes in a neat pile for Monique or Helena to collect, retrieved her stethoscope from the back of her chair and laced it around her neck. She picked up a thermometer and dropped it into the top pocket of her shirt, then marched outside ahead of him to the ward block where she retrieved her *chaderi* from her office.

She threaded it over her head as they walked. 'Did you get lunch?' She hadn't, but she hadn't had much of an appetite today. 'Do you want something to eat before we go?'

'No.' He followed her to the Jeep.

Tessa chattered about all sorts of things on the way into town—about the cases she'd seen that afternoon, about the supplies that should have arrived by now, about the things she was planning to order for the next delivery, about everything that entered her head—everything except anything that concerned James.

He barely spoke.

They were stopped at one roadblock and waved through the next. There was another checkpoint, a new one, just before they entered the market square. It was as quiet as the last time she'd been in town, as far as civilians went, though today there was a heavy militia presence in the square. Dozens of armed soldiers lounged in vehicles, including two tanks, around it.

She directed James away from the streets that had been damaged in the bomb attack and through back streets to the house where Ahmad's family lived.

The toddler seemed delighted to see them, running squealing towards Tessa when his grandmother opened the door to them.

He giggled as James examined his abdomen. 'Completely normal,' said James calmly when he'd finished, taking the thermometer Tessa produced and putting it into his pocket before she could bring it anywhere near the child. 'There's nothing wrong with him,' he said easily. 'Stop looking for trouble.'

They stayed for tea—in a Sadakhi household it was an insult not to.

When they returned to the Jeep James started the engine, then waited. 'Any other wild goose chases I should know about?'

'Home, James,' she said and, unable to stop herself, she laughed. 'I've been wanting to say that since you first arrived.'

'Idiot.' But he smiled. 'You must have known that child would be perfectly fine.'

'I still needed to check.' But the visit had taken longer than she'd expected and she peered anxiously at the sun. Already red, it was sinking. Fast. 'Now hurry, James,' she ordered, only half-joking. 'The shooting starts at dark.'

'Now she tells me.' He shoved the vehicle into reverse, wincing at the grinding sound it always made. 'Although, with all those roadblocks and all those soldiers, I think we should be safe enough.'

'Not as safe as you think—they're the ones who'll be shooting.' She met his sharp look with a pale smile. 'True,' she said lightly. 'Sorry.'

They were rounding the corner of the square now and Tessa frowned as they approached the first checkpoint. Earlier it had been manned by just two soldiers but now there were at least a dozen.

Cursing herself for leaving the hospital empty-handed, she said, 'Got any money on you?'

'About fifty dollars.'

'We might need it.'

A soldier in his teens, his Kalashnikov pointed at the Jeep where before it'd been worn carelessly across his chest, stepped onto the road and held up one hand.

James stopped and Tessa greeted the boy, conscious that his colleagues seemed tense and watchful beside them. She held out their passports, explaining that they'd been visiting a sick child in the town.

He took the passports, then flicked silently through each one, studying every page. Without speaking, he lifted his gun to indicate that James should get out of the Jeep.

'Do it,' she said quietly. 'For God's sake, don't try anything macho or you'll get us both shot. Act like he's the boss.'

'Are you kidding?' James shot her a dryly incredulous look as he climbed out. 'With that thing he *is* the boss.'

'We are doctors from the hospital,' she explained when the boy bent in to inspect James's side of the vehicle. She knew he'd already know where they were from—they were the only foreigners within hundreds of miles—but it seemed important to keep him talking.

'In my country doctors are paid very well,' he said roughly, straightening again, the gun pointed at James.

'We are not paid well,' she countered. 'We are poor. Our money goes to the sick.'

'In my country soldiers are poorly paid,' the boy continued. 'Sometimes they have no money for many seasons.'

'That is bad,' she said. 'There should be money for everyone, especially for those who defend our safety.'

James shifted, stilling when the soldier's attention swung back to him and the gun lifted again. 'What's he saying?'

'He wants money.'

'Tell him he can have it!'

'Not yet.' Tessa hadn't taken her eyes off the boy. 'My friend is concerned,' she said gently. 'There are many sick people in our hospital and we are not with them. If our papers are in order may we leave?'

'Your papers are in order.' He dropped the passports onto James's seat. 'Do not come out after dark again,' he warned roughly, lowering his gun. 'There are bandits—it is not safe here.'

'You are good-hearted and wise.' She lowered her head, her pulse thudding hard in her ears. 'James, get in.'

The boy returned to his colleagues and watched them as James started the Jeep.

James shot a quick look back at them as they accelerated away, then flicked on the headlights and said, 'Why didn't you want to pay him?'

'One, possibly two roadblocks to go,' she said, surprised by how matter-of-fact she sounded. In all the years she'd been at the hospital that was only the second time she'd felt any sense of personal unease at a roadblock— the first time had been the last time she'd visited Ahmad. 'They'll have radioed ahead,' she continued. 'They'll know we're coming.'

They were approaching the edge of town now, still about a mile and a half from the hospital. The sun was down, red and yellow streaks of light splintering across the western sky the only trace left of day against the blackness of the rest of the sky. It was cooling down, too, and the night breeze chilled her arms, bare beneath her robe.

'Slow down,' she said, leaning forward and squinting through the netting in her gown. 'They're just beyond that ridge.'

Two soldiers waited on the road with arms outstretched, guns on their hips. James stopped and Tessa produced their passports and explained again who they were and what they'd been doing in the town.

But Tessa could see they weren't interested and she suspected she was right to have assumed that the other soldiers would have radioed their colleagues because they waved the passports away, not even wanting to see them. Before she could finish telling them about the hospital the boy on the right, the smaller of the two, ordered them both from the vehicle.

Suddenly realising what was going to happen, and even though James had already climbed out, Tessa gripped the side of her seat and the edge of her door, not moving. 'We need it,' she said urgently. 'We must have transport for the sick. We must have transport for our supplies.'

'Our need is greater.' The boy was unmoved. He waited. 'Please remove yourself.'

Tessa didn't budge. 'It is not a good vehicle,' she insisted. 'It will not serve you well.'

The other boy's gun came up, pointing directly at her chest.

'Think of the sick and the dying. How can we treat them without our vehicle?'

The boy looked angry now and, behind her, James swore.

Proving that he'd understood what was going on and ignoring the soldiers' warning shouts and the guns that had swivelled to his own chest, he stormed around to her side of the vehicle, reached under her and scooped her out of her seat. 'It's only a bloody car,' he said violently when she struggled with him. 'Are you mad?'

'Shut up,' she snarled. 'We need it.'

'We need you, too, and me,' he grated as he carried her out of the way and lowered her to the ground at the edge of the road, holding her there as the boys climbed into the Jeep and started it. 'Leave it.'

His hand gripped her arm and she could do nothing anyway so she stayed still, watching forlornly as the soldiers—grinning like naughty children—revved the ancient engine and then spun the vehicle around and hurtled away back down the road towards town.

'Mohammed will be furious,' she said sadly. 'That was his treasure.'

'Mohammed will be pleased you're alive,' James said tersely.

'Don't hold your breath.' Tessa stayed still, waiting for her eyes to adjust to the starlit darkness now that the lights of the Jeep were retreating. 'They might have left but there could still be another roadblock to get through.'

'It's dark,' he said flatly. 'We can skirt around it.'

'Too many mines. It's more dangerous to leave the road.' Her eyes having now become accustomed to the darkness, she could make out the pale strip of road ahead of them, and she started walking. 'To threaten us like that they must really be scared,' she mused. 'That or desperate for money. Perhaps it's true and that they haven't been paid. Did you notice how young they were?'

'I only noticed the weapons,' James countered dryly, walking beside her. 'One of those adds a decade or two.'

'They've lost their boyhoods.' She stumbled on a loose rock and he grabbed for her, catching her arm and then her hand to support her. It was warm and strong and comforted her, and she gripped him, not letting him take it away again. 'We do need the Jeep, though. I don't know how we'll manage without it.'

'I'll buy you another one.' His grip on her hand tightened briefly. 'You should have taken the BMW,' he added softly. 'It was a better offer.'

'I didn't think you meant it.' They trudged for a while in silence, the gentle padding of their feet and the swell-

ing buzz of night insects the only noise. 'Are you so
terribly rich, James?'

Despite the darkness that made his outline a dim shape,
she sensed him looking at her. 'Not all of my own
making,' he admitted quietly. 'My grandfather enjoyed
art. He was a wise collector.'

'Ah.' She smiled, understanding. 'Hence the Picasso.'

James growled. 'Remember what curiosity did to the
cat?' he rasped.

But Tessa found herself laughing. 'I couldn't resist it,'
she admitted. 'Sorry.'

'Liar.' But his voice was thick with amusement and
she realised that he didn't mind that she'd peeked into
his bedroom. 'What were you expecting to see?'

'Oh, a king-size water-bed and mirrors on the ceiling,'
she chirped. 'Champagne coolers and an enormous spa
bath—those sorts of things.'

James laughed, and the hand which had held hers
slid around her waist, hugging her to him. 'So I
disappointed you?'

'Not at all.' His room had been masculine but plain
and, apart from the Picasso, not at all opulent. 'I liked it.'

'Then you'll have to visit it again.' His voice had
deepened and he stopped, swivelling her to face him. He
lifted the stethoscope from around her neck and hung it
around his own. 'Take that off,' he said gently, and she
felt his hands tugging at the fabric of her *chaderi*.
'Will you?'

'Will I take it off?' she asked.

'Will you visit me?' More adroit than she'd realised,
he already had the gown gathered at her neck.

'No.' She shivered as he tugged the garment over her
head, although whether it was from the cold against her
arms or from James's touch she wasn't sure. 'Next time
I'm in London I'm staying in a hotel,' she declared, her
heart hammering as hard as it had at the roadblock. 'I
think it would be safer.'

'It would definitely be safer,' he confirmed softly,

coming closer to nuzzle her cheek. 'But would it be quite as much fun?'

'James. . .?'

His mouth felt its way to the corner of hers. 'Hmm?'

'We're a mile from the hospital,' she whispered. 'It's dark. We have no vehicle and hardly any money. There might be armed soldiers ahead of us—and there certainly are behind us—and we're surrounded by mines.'

'And you're enchanting.' He kissed her properly, opened her mouth with his and possessed her.

He was warm and urgent and the clean familiarity of his scent surrounded her. Involuntarily her head fell back, and James deepened his kiss approvingly. Pressed against the hardness of him and cushioned from the night around them, his mouth was urgent and demanding on hers. She closed her eyes, begging for strength to fight the swell of desire that threatened to overwhelm her.

'This is insane,' she murmured, unable to stop her faint protest when his mouth lifted. She rose on tiptoe, opening her mouth, although her brain was shrieking at her to push away from him and her body was stiff.

James bit softly at her chin. 'Stop fighting me,' he urged, gathering her barely resisting body closer into his so that she could feel his desire. 'You're always fighting me.'

'I don't have any choice.' It was like a groan. But her fingers dug into the hard flesh of his shoulders, disobeying the orders from her head, and she didn't try and escape when she felt him start to unfasten her shirt. 'James. . .'

'Tessa.' His voice was quiet and determined, determined like the hands that seemed intent on baring her. 'I want to see you.'

'But it's dark,' she protested, his words startling her. She grabbed his hands to still them and held her shirt closed, struggling to stay rational. They were on a road, a dangerous road, and they weren't safe. 'Not now.'

'Now,' he insisted, his mouth on hers again, unerringly

this time—his tongue rough, then gentle, probing, playing with her, tempting her—while his hands slowly worked at hers, loosening her grip on her shirt. 'We both want this, Tessa. Nothing else matters. We don't know what's ahead of us here. There might never be another time for us.'

He was right, she realised, faint at the thought. Nothing today had been normal—anything could happen to them. It was dark and, although she'd tried to hide it, she was frightened of what lay ahead. James was her comfort and she needed him.

Abruptly she weakened, acknowledging that at this moment in her life when there were no other considerations she wanted to be with him.

Letting go of her shirt because it no longer seemed important to protect herself, she let herself soften, fall against him and give herself up to the urgent heat of his embrace.

But something about him—some faint, almost surprised stillness before he welcomed her, kissed her again and before the warmth of his hands slid to her breasts—alerted her.

Bracing her hands against his chest she pushed back and twisted herself free to glare at the dim shadow that was him. 'What did you say?'

'I said we might not get another chance,' he said softly, pulling her forward again.

But this time she didn't let him. That line was straight out of one of those old war movies she'd watched as a child. 'You...you...How could you say that?' she hissed. 'This isn't some sort of game!'

'It was worth a try.' And instead of protesting, instead of arguing his sincerity, James laughed at her. 'The opportunity was too good,' he said unrepentantly, laughing harder as he fended off the small fists that hammered at him randomly. 'Stop it, Tessa. You'll hurt yourself.'

'I'll hurt you,' she cried, outraged. 'How dare you?'

'How could I not?' James caught her hands, hauled

her into his arms and kissed her soundly, forcing her to be silent. 'God, you're gorgeous when you're mad.'

'You can't see me,' she said weakly, cursing his charm and furious at his utter desirability.

'But I can feel you.' His voice changed. Gone was the teasing—now it was low and grating and it made her shiver. 'And I wasn't entirely playing, not at first.' But he put her away from him. He put her away and he buttoned her shirt all the way to the top, then crouched, stood and handed her her *chaderi*, helping her to feed it over her head. 'Come on. It's not safe. Let's go.'

'I felt sorry for you,' she said quietly as they walked.

'That's sweet.'

She stopped. 'But I wouldn't have gone through with it.'

'Of course you wouldn't.' He took her hand again and tucked it into his elbow. His voice was serious but she felt his amusement like a blanket around her. 'I believe you.'

'All right, I would have,' she whispered, honesty forcing her to admit the truth they both understood. 'I thought if I was about to die there was nothing to lose.'

'I'm not planning on dying tonight,' he said quietly. 'Thanks all the same.'

'It's not that I think sex with you wouldn't be good.'

'Hush.' James kissed the top of her gowned head. Somewhere, far behind them, there was the sound of a rapid round of shooting, then another. 'Let's just get out of here, hmm?'

He tugged her forward and tugged a little harder when she resisted him. 'Come on, Tessa,' he urged. 'I only meant to take your mind off the danger, not make you take more risks. Move.'

'I'm moving.' She stalked off. 'Why aren't you married?'

'Why are you curious?'

'I'm just interested.' Tessa knew how women fluttered around him. Even Richard, never short of admirers himself, had been jealous of James's magnetism. 'You've probably been spoilt for choice.'

'More likely spending too much time at work.' He didn't sound particularly interested. A few paces further on his hand tightened. 'Isn't this where the road-block was?'

'About here.' They stopped and looked around. It was too dark for her to see much beyond the border of the road, but all seemed quiet. 'They probably left before dark,' she declared. 'Or they're guarding the airport.'

'Or they're at the hospital.' James looked ahead to the lights. 'Would they go there?'

'They never have before.' But things had happened today that had never happened before and they began to hurry, jogging the last hundred yards or so.

Mohammed was at the entrance, obviously watching for them, his expression dark with concern as he waited for them to run up to him. Once Mohammed had reassured them that there'd been no hostile visits from soldiers, James explained about the Jeep.

Rather than being upset, as Tessa had expected, Mohammed's shrug was philosophical. 'They are young and ready to fight, and angry because there is no money for them,' he explained, confirming Tessa's suspicions that the soldiers hadn't been paid. 'Tomorrow, perhaps, they will return it to us. They will not be allowed to keep it. You will see.'

The older man looked at James as they walked towards the mess. 'And she has made you hurry, James.' He clicked his tongue. 'That is unfortunate.'

'Tessa wasn't making me hurry,' James said, with a quick grin in her direction. There was another distant burst of gunfire. 'That was.'

'Only playing tonight.' Mohammed looked unworried. 'Firing at the sky. Nothing serious.'

The others didn't share Mohammed's calm reaction to the loss of the Jeep. Axel, in particular, was furious. 'I would have fought them,' he declared, using a broom handle to demonstrate his sword-fighting skills. 'Threaten me, you ruffians?' He mock-battled Tessa around the mess, making her laugh. 'Never! Die first.'

'I can see it now.' Helena rolled her eyes. 'You. Two seconds later. Dead.'

'I'm sure James was very brave.' Monique fluttered her lashes in his direction. 'Weren't you, James?'

'No.' James smiled at Tessa. 'Not at all.'

'Then you are sensible.' Helena gave them both tea. 'Things are changing here, Tessa.'

Tessa sighed, knowing it was true but not knowing what she could do about it.

After dinner she took James to her office for his first language lesson. She wasn't entirely sure he'd take the teaching seriously but it seemed he was genuinely interested in learning and, apart from an occasional assessing look that made her flush, he applied himself seriously to the session.

They worked for an hour on the spoken word only, having agreed that the written alphabet, as it was Arabic not Roman, was too major a task for the time available.

She was impressed by the amount he'd already picked up in his brief time in the country. 'You have an ear for it,' she declared as they walked slowly back towards the mess. 'It was months before I picked up as many words as you have.'

'It's my teacher,' James said softly, his arm sliding around her waist as they strolled. 'She fills me with... enthusiasm.'

Glad of the darkness which hid her flush, Tessa disengaged his arm and increased her pace, flustered by the soft laughter that followed her through the night.

CHAPTER NINE

Two days later Mohammed came to see Tessa and James in Theatre. 'The Jeep has returned,' he said serenely. 'This morning. In the front of the hospital. Completely unharmed.'

There was a round of relieved sighs and Tessa looked up from the thigh wound they were exploring. 'No message?'

'The vehicle is message enough,' Mohammed answered.

The wound she was exploring was one she'd debrided several days earlier. She syringed its depths with saline, collected a small blood clot that had worked loose and dumped it into a rubbish bag.

Mohammed was right, she acknowledged. The return of the vehicle was significant. It showed that there was not yet total anarchy here—that the soldiers were still under the control of a disciplinary force—and it reaffirmed that the hospital was not considered a legitimate target for aggression.

Probing the wound with her gloved fingers and feeling gently for any debris she might have missed earlier, Tessa glanced up again and caught a pointed look Axel was directing at James.

Merrily, the anaesthetist said, 'May I suggest no further romantic evening excursions in our hospital vehicle?'

Helena, who was scrubbing for them this session, laughed, rolling her eyes when Tessa looked at her.

'We were visiting Ahmad,' Tessa said crisply, ignoring James's mockingly knowing look—grateful that the last two days had been so busy that he'd had no opportunity to taunt her about her response to his embrace the night

131

the Jeep had been commandeered. 'Work, Axel, work. A concept you probably don't understand.'

'Ah, how she jokes,' Axel said sweetly, turning the page of the lurid-looking novel he was reading while he supervised the anaesthetic. 'I who slave like a servant.'

'Like a servant in a book shop,' Tessa argued.

Axel sniffed. 'The best anaesthetist in the northern hemisphere should be well read.'

James laughed. 'The best anaesthetist in the northern hemisphere should be watching his pressures,' he said easily, nodding towards one of the gauges on the machine which had swung almost to empty. 'Aren't you missing something?'

'Fear not,' pronounced Axel, and laid aside his book as Mohammed returned, lugging a large cylinder which he proceeded to substitute for the one James had indicated. 'Attention to your assistant, famous surgeon. This end is under my control.'

'I'm not the assistant,' Tessa grumbled, experimentally pulling the edges of the wound together to see if she would be able to close without putting any tension upon the skin. 'I'm the surgeon here. James is *my* assistant.'

'Undermine another half-centimetre,' James instructed softly, his eyes dancing as they met hers—effortlessly proving her announcement to be prematurely boastful. 'That's too tight.'

Silently she followed his suggestion and gently freed a rim of skin all around the wound from its adhering tissues, allowing the wound to close effortlessly.

She used interrupted nylon stitches to close, stood back to allow Helena to cover the wound with a light pressure dressing, then applied a splint to the thigh to keep the limb immobilised for healing.

'That looked good,' she said to James, as they scrubbed again. 'Didn't you think? He should recover reasonable strength in those quadriceps.'

'With work.' Using his elbow, James dispensed more iodine solution onto his palms, lathering it into a froth before soaping his arms. 'He'll always have a defect there but he'll walk all right.' He leaned down to rinse at the same time as she did. 'How are you set up for physio?'

'I'd trade six months' supply of peanut butter for a trained one,' she said easily, knowing that by now he would understand the enormity of that sacrifice. 'But we get by. Our patients are highly motivated; they work hard to get their strength back. They have to. There's no social security here. If they can't perform the role that's allocated to them they lose everything.'

She wiped her hands dry with a sterile cloth before she opened out a gown, smiling her thanks as Axel came to tie it. 'You watch with Fath,' she said, referring to their next case—the boy whose leg she'd had to amputate after the rocket attack. 'He'll be up and about as soon as we take the sutures out.'

She walked towards the operating trolley where Axel already had their patient anaesthetised, then hesitated, not sure on which side to stand.

'I'll assist,' said James easily, directing her to the right. 'There's no hurry today.'

She smiled her thanks, knowing it must be tedious for him this way but grateful for the training he was giving her. 'Hello, Axel,' she said lightly. 'Me again.'

Rather than the grumbles she'd expected, Axel shrugged. 'You're getting faster,' he said, surprising her because she hadn't realised.

She stayed with James all morning, then went to clinic where Mohammed and Khan joined her. A sulking Monique, obviously unhappy that Helena had insisted on spending the day in Theatre, appeared later.

Tessa registered Monique's injured feelings with a sigh, but Monique had been monopolising the scrubbing duties since James's arrival and short of overriding Helena, which she wasn't prepared to do, there was nothing she could change.

'But I wish to improve my theatre skills,' Monique

protested. 'Helena is very experienced in this way—she doesn't need to work there.'

'This is her first full day in two weeks,' Tessa said gently. 'And I need you here. You're wonderful with the children. They love you.'

'I know.' Appearing faintly mollified, the nurse managed a small smile. 'But James works so well with me. I'm sure he must be missing my help. Perhaps I should go and see?'

'James will just have to cope,' she said firmly. 'You're needed here.'

'I'm always needed everywhere.' The nurse heaved a large sigh, her shoulders lifting with the effort of it all. 'It's only that when we are alone he begs me to work with him,' she said, startling Tessa. 'I think he finds Helena too slow.'

Monique closed the door on her way out and Tessa stared at it, mystified. Helena was a fast and efficient worker—the complaint was completely unjustified.

Late that afternoon after clinic the noise of a small plane, circling above the hospital, sent Tessa hurrying outside. She waited impatiently for Mohammed to join her at the Jeep and when he finally came James was with him.

James took the Jeep with her, while Mohammed followed behind in an even older four-wheel drive that he'd borrowed from his cousin to help with the delivery. *En route*, Tessa questioned James about Monique's comments.

'The woman's mad,' he said bluntly, swerving to avoid a hole and sending a shower of dust in Mohammed's direction as he accelerated ahead. 'She's making it up.'

'But if you prefer to work with Monique—?'

'I'm studying the language,' he said impatiently. 'Would I be doing that if I wanted to work only with her?'

'I suppose not,' she said slowly. But still she hesitated. Perhaps Monique had misunderstood whatever he'd said? 'James, you'd speak to me rather than Monique if you really wanted things run differently, wouldn't you?'

James swore. Without warning, he slammed on the brakes and stopped the Jeep in a shower of sand and stones. 'Tessa Mathesson, you may drive me to madness,' he said roughly. And he kissed her, a hard, demanding adult kiss that made her tremble.

When he lifted his head blue-grey eyes bore into her dazed wide green ones with an impatience she could taste. 'Your time is fast running out. Do you understand me?'

'Mohammed. . .?' He was still behind them because he drove far slower than James but Mohammed's Jeep was catching up, and she swivelled her head, dizzy from James's kiss but still aware enough to be concerned. 'James, Mohammed—'

'I don't care.' His hand gripped her chin, not allowing her to look away again. 'They all know what we both want. You're the only one trying to ignore it.'

'I'm hoping it'll go away,' she said faintly, sliding back into her seat as he released her with a disgusted sigh and put the Jeep into gear.

'Believe me, it doesn't.' James's mouth set tight and he raced towards the airport gate.

When he stopped at the entrance Tessa handed the guards their customary gifts, wearily adding a few extra notes when they protested about their poor wages.

The plane was about to land and James parked at the edge of the runway and stopped the engine. 'What exactly do you have in mind for yourself, Tessa? A life of celibacy?'

The words startled her and she stiffened, her eyes on the plane but realising that, beyond knowing she needed to resist James, she hadn't given the issue much thought. 'I don't know,' she admitted, shouting over the noise of the aircraft's engine. 'I suppose.'

Mohammed had now arrived, and the plane was slowing. James looked at her broodingly as he swung himself out of the Jeep. 'Fifty years,' he called, over the noise of the taxiing engine. 'Maybe sixty. That's a long time.'

The little plane bore more than the large order she'd placed because the agency, possibly having heard about the troop movements around the capital and the whispers of war, had included several extra boxes of emergency supplies and blankets that she hadn't ordered, but which she was grateful for.

Consequently it took them more than the customary fifteen minutes to unload the plane, and she kept a wary watch on the guards' hut while she gave the pilot their mail bag and he exchanged it for the one he'd brought. Then they moved back to the vehicles, waiting for him to take off again.

The extra money she'd paid had clearly kept the soldiers happy, though, because there were no demands for customs papers and inspections or any of the other nonsense the soldiers sometimes requested as they drove out.

She travelled with James again, but Mohammed had left first so they were forced to drive very slowly, keeping distance between them to allow his dust to settle before they caught up.

'About the fifty years.' She didn't look at him but kept her eyes fixed on the shapes of the town far to their left, sure that he was probably grinning. 'Nuns manage it.'

They were starting to catch up with the dust again and, instead of slowing, James stopped the Jeep. 'Is that how you see yourself?'

'No.'

'Sure?'

'Positive.' But looking at him was a mistake because she saw that he wasn't laughing at her, not at all—he was deadly serious. 'I don't understand why this is so important to you,' she protested.

'It's important because I can't look at you and think of anything else,' he said quietly. 'If you want it stripped to basics then I guess that's how it is.'

She couldn't sustain the challenge in his eyes and looked away. 'It's just sex.'

'Then let's get it out of the way.'

'It's not that simple for me.' She folded her arms, staring ahead. 'Men are so different—'

'Don't.' James's palm slammed down onto the steering-wheel, bringing her gaze skittering back to him. 'Don't compare me to any other men you've known.'

'There's just been Richard,' she said dully, grimacing as she registered the irony of him telling her not to compare him to Richard when, of course, it was his difference from him that frightened her most. If James was like her husband she'd at least have an inkling about how to handle him.

James's eyes had darkened. 'Richard was the first?'

'And only.' She stared at the cloud which was Mohammed's Jeep. 'Mohammed is way ahead,' she said tightly. 'We can go now.'

'Soon.' He touched her hair, a light, fleeting touch that puzzled her. 'That surprises me. When Richard and I first met you you seemed so confident, worldly almost. I assumed you were more experienced than that.'

'You don't have to be a sex maniac to be confident,' she said stiffly.

'Sex maniac?' His grin was lazily amused and it disarmed her. 'Hardly. How old were you then? Twenty-three? Four?'

'I suppose.'

'Old enough to have had a number of partners.'

'Well, I hadn't.' Tessa shifted, uneasy. She could discuss sex with him, even sometimes enjoy such. . .adult talk because it was novel for her—novel and exciting. But what she wasn't liking was the reminder of when they'd all met.

It didn't help her to remember that in the beginning it hadn't been Richard who'd made her pulse race.

She stilled, finally allowing herself to recognise the stark, shocking truth that she'd started to acknowledge the evening in her office when James had revealed he'd understood about her marriage.

In the beginning, in the very beginning, when she'd begun working with both of them it had been James, not Richard, who'd attracted her. The memories she'd banished to the depths of her mind surfaced abruptly. In fact, she'd barely noticed Richard, so hard had James impacted on her senses.

But she'd been inexperienced, unable to reconcile her reaction to James with the plans she'd made for her future. And Richard had been there and he was friendly and cheerful, infinitely more approachable than his more guarded colleague, and she could relax with him and so she'd begun to spend time with him.

It hadn't taken her long to discover that Richard shared her enthusiasm about working somewhere like Sadakh, an enthusiasm that was central to her own life and that had forged a bond between them that she hadn't anticipated. And Richard had had a vulnerability about him that she'd been wise enough to realise James hadn't shared, a vulnerability and need for her approval that had made her care for him.

Tessa felt a brief, unexpected rush of warmth for the man who'd become her husband, a fondness she hadn't felt since the moment he'd told her what had happened with Monique—a revelation which had finally driven her to tell him to leave.

Unlike Richard, James seemed to her to be totally solid and invulnerable. She met him as an equal and she acknowledged that now, now that she was wiser and understood herself better, that made him powerfully compelling for her.

But comparing the two men made her feel disloyal and she stared ahead to the distant shape of the hospital buildings. 'I couldn't have done this without him,' she said faintly.

'Yes, you could.' James seemed to understand what she was saying. 'The strength came from you. I was always surprised he came. This was your dream, not his.'

'Not in the beginning.' At first Richard had wanted this, too. He'd worked as hard as she had and, stimulated by the work and the chance to practise the craft he excelled at, he'd given everything he could. But for him the dream had eventually faded. His involvement with Monique had just been a symptom of his need to escape, but in the end the choice had been hers for Richard had been incapable of making such a decision alone.

But still she could have saved her marriage if she'd left Sadakh with him. 'I chose to stay here,' she told James. 'Perhaps I'll always choose to stay here. For now, this is where I belong.'

'That's the second time you've said that.' There were a few tight, silent moments then he said softly, 'I know that, Tessa. I don't want to change that or change you— I want to make love to you. They're different things. Does this have to be treated so seriously?'

Seriously? Tessa blinked at him. It was serious, wasn't it? But his gentleness softened her and she hesitated. She was an adult. She...desired him. And if afterwards it hurt then that was part of life, wasn't it? She was only hesitating because she was frightened of a little emotional pain. Given the pain she saw every day around her, wasn't that more than a little melodramatic?

Still unsure, she sent him a doubtful, sideways look. 'Just my body, hmm?'

'Please.'

James's sudden grin shattered her introspection, made her doubts seem silly, made her laugh.

'Is this another of your bedding techniques?'

'Probably.'

'I can't believe I'm falling for this.' She rolled her eyes, but of course she was. 'What did you have in mind? One night?'

'Whatever it takes.' He leaned towards her and kissed her hard on the cheek. Then he started the Jeep and drove off. 'Good girl.'

'James. . .?' Her fingers curled around the edges of the Jeep's frame. 'Don't expect me to be very good at this.'

'Relax, Tessa.' He sent her a quick, amused look. 'You're not sitting an exam.'

When they reached the hospital she helped him to unload, flushing each time they brushed against each other, supremely conscious of him. She crouched among the boxes, ticking off items against the invoice, before she instructed the others about where to deliver each package.

Axel returned from his third deposit, grumbling about James's whistling. 'I am the cheerful one among us,' he declared. 'That is my role. If there is to be whistling then I am to be doing it.'

Tessa shoved two boxes full of ampoules of anaesthetic agents at him. 'Your precious Ketamine's there,' she said, hoping that would keep him quiet. 'And enough Thiopentone to last you six months.'

'Rejoice.' Axel danced away, beaming.

'You have made his day for him.' Helena accepted a carton of swabs for Theatre. 'James is happy, too. How nice to work with two such happy men.'

Tessa ignored her. 'Where's Monique?' Supply day was generally the highlight of the month for everyone. 'She'd like to see all this.'

'Monique has a headache.' Helena shrugged. 'She is in bed. She wanted a doctor. She asked for James but I sent Axel. I don't think she is happy.'

'I'll go and see her.' Tessa frowned at the nurse. 'Helena, have a little patience with Monique—'

'I know. I know.' Helena waved her away. 'I try, Tessa, but I am not a saint like you.'

A saint? Tessa's mouth twisted as Helena tripped away. Hardly.

But the mail that had come with the supplies alleviated some of her doubts in that direction for, along with the usual pile of letters from her family and the agency and

her various sponsors and contributors, there was a large,
formal-looking envelope with a Seattle postmark.

Leaving the others—with James's dark gaze prickling
her back—she picked up the envelope and went to
her room.

The letter was long and flowery in Richard's usual
style, but the point was clear. He'd met a woman—a
young woman, only twenty—and he wanted to marry
her. Soon. He enclosed papers for her to sign to dissolve
the marriage, a confident assurance that since his new job
was extremely profitable and his fiancée independently
wealthy he was happy to continue to send his current
contribution for the hospital for as long as she needed
it, a birthday card for the birthday he'd forgotten four
months earlier and a photograph of him with his new
girlfriend.

Tessa sank back onto her bed and lay flat, staring
at the ceiling for what seemed like hours before she
remembered Monique's headache. She rolled over and
off the bed and went to see her.

The pain was improving. 'I took two paracetamol,'
Monique said miserably. 'They make me sick.'

'Perhaps if you manage some dinner. . .?'

'I have no hunger.' The nurse rolled onto her side,
facing away from Tessa. 'I am too ill.'

'OK.' Tessa backed to the door.

'I think I should like to work in Theatre tomorrow,'
Monique said, as Tessa was about to leave. 'If I am
better. With James. Is this possible?'

'I guess.' For the sake of peace Tessa decided she was
not prepared to argue the point with Helena. 'I'll come
and see you later.'

'James can come, if he wants,' the nurse said quickly.

'He's busy,' Tessa said gently, sensing that James
would not appreciate the invitation. 'Unpacking the
supplies.'

'Oh.' Monique covered her head with a sheet.

When she joined the others for dinner she explained

about Monique being unwell. 'Helena, I wondered if you'd help me tomorrow on the wards and let Monique scrub for James. Is that all right?'

'Fine.' But Helena's regard was shrewd. 'Is the headache any better?'

'I think so. It's not a migraine.' She dished some rice mixed with coriander and carrots onto her plate. 'Mohammed, I missed Ali in clinic today. He should have come for his medicine. Did you see him?'

'I administered his injection,' he confirmed. 'Are you happy with that?'

'Yes.' Tessa nodded; Mohammed was as able to administer the medication as she was. 'Just wanted to check that he came. If we don't have any more emergencies, perhaps we should admit him again for a week or so.'

She ate her food, aware of James's probing gaze on her but wary of returning it.

Over tea she opened some more mail, reading her parents' and siblings' cheerful descriptions of their lives with her usual faint feeling of disbelief. Descriptions of dinner parties and shopping trips and children's birthday parties always seemed surreal and absurd when she was in Sadakh.

One of the agency's memos contained a surprise. 'No surgeon yet,' she told the others, 'but they're interviewing a casualty and ICU-trained nurse who's applied to come out. He's worked in Somalia and Mozambique.' She straightened, interested, then checked the date with Axel's watch. 'They've interviewed him already,' she added. 'Yesterday. I wonder when we'll find out?'

'When he arrives.' Helena laughed. 'Remember Monique? We didn't even know they were interviewing her.'

'Hmm.' Tessa consoled herself with the fact that at least this person had had field experience. He was in his thirties—old enough to understand more about what he was getting into.

James said, 'No news at all about a surgeon?'

'Nothing.' Tessa looked at him. 'We'll cope,' she said quietly. 'Every day I spend with you I learn more.'

'It's not enough.' He put his own letters down and stood up, his expression grim. 'You can't be expected to manage alone.'

'It's not your problem.' She turned back to her letters and when she looked up again James had gone.

Later she went to the wards, and when she came back James was alone in the darkened mess. He was sprawled in the easy chair, a glass of Scotch in his hand and the cordial bottle at his feet.

She stopped in the door, watching him warily. Their talk in the Jeep this afternoon suddenly seemed almost a world away. 'Not tonight, James.'

'Relax, Tessa.' He sounded tired and the eyes that lifted briefly to hers were guarded and shadowed. 'I'm not exactly in the mood myself.'

Lowering her head, she walked quickly away to her bed.

Helena shook her awake during the night. 'Another rocket attack. Casualties coming.'

Tessa was up instantly and the two women ran across to the hospital together. 'I cannot believe the noise you can sleep through,' Helena panted. 'We have all been up for hours.'

'Years of training,' Tessa shouted. As a paediatric registrar she'd learned to snatch sleep whenever she could. She could sleep through anything but a bleeper and there was no need for a paging system here.

The hospital itself was still quiet but there was thundering and sounds of automatic weapon fire in the distance. 'Mohammed and James have taken the Jeeps,' Helena told her. 'Ours and Mohammed's cousin's.'

'What?'

Perhaps noting Tessa's abrupt pallor, Helena said carefully, 'The militia from Hafeez's village have struck their neighbours. It's a small village and you know they only have two vehicles there. They couldn't cope alone with the casualties.'

'But that's too dangerous.'

'They've gone.' Helena directed Tessa to the store-room, pushing her towards a stack of boxes where some of the supplies from the new delivery had still not been unpacked. 'Theatre's ready and the technicians are in the lab,' she said firmly. 'We have to take emergency things with us to triage and Theatre—supplies are low.'

'Adrenaline, lignocaine.' Mechanically Tessa pushed the boxes of ampoules to one side, leaving the drugs they were less likely to require in the cartons.

The sound of rockets and firing was a constant back-ground roar but she flinched at an especially loud explosion, hesitating a few seconds before returning to her task. 'When did they leave?'

'Thirty, forty minutes ago.' Helena squeezed her arm. She bundled the medications they'd sorted into an empty box and lifted it into her arms. 'Monique's scrubbing. Axel's in Theatre. I'll cover triage with some of the other nurses. You'd better go and scrub.'

The first casualty arrived in Theatre as she finished scrubbing. It was a young boy, unconscious, his lower right leg blasted into fragments.

Axel smoothly emptied a syringe into the line that was already running saline into his arm. 'All right, Tessa.'

'Antibiotics and tetanus?'

'Given.'

Tessa worked mechanically to stem the bleeding then amputated at the lower femur. She left the nurse who was assisting her to complete the dressings and explored the wound on his other leg, cleaned it but left it open, covered by gauze dressings and loosely bandaged.

Her next case was waiting in the other theatre—a middle-aged woman with abdominal and chest injuries. She was still conscious, wailing and crying and demanding to know where her son was. She clutched at

Axel's arm as he murmured a few words of comfort and swiftly instilled the anaesthetic along with pain relief. When her grip relaxed into sleep he hauled back her gown so Tessa could assess her injuries.

The chest wounds were bloody but not penetrating and Axel confirmed that she had good breath sounds bilaterally so Tessa covered the wounds with gauze, then a pressure dressing and started on the abdomen.

The shrapnel had ripped through her skin and torn her small bowel but there wasn't any other organ damage so Tessa quickly excised the damaged bowel and sewed over a couple of tiny perforations then instilled anti-worm antibiotic around the excision margins, before suturing the healthy tissues together. After washing out the peritoneum she closed it, then tackled the skin wounds, packed where she didn't want to suture and covered the whole area with broad dressings.

She returned to the chest wounds. The bleeding had stopped and she cleaned the wounds, excised some severely injured muscle and the skin margins, then covered them with more gauze, leaving the skin open.

When she returned from changing her blood-drenched gown her third patient was being wheeled into the clean theatre—another young boy with massive leg injuries but this time still conscious although drowsy.

Axel bent over to examine the patient's head which, she could see, had also been injured. Axel said a few words and the boy's eyes closed. Tessa saw Axel frown and she tensed. The anaesthetist lifted the boy's eyelids and then straightened, obviously alarmed.

'His right pupil's dilating.'

'Oh, God.' Not worrying that she was de-sterilising herself, Tessa whirled back to the other room where the kit to open a child's skull was kept.

The change in his pupil suggested that a blood clot was building up against his brain and damaging the nerves as it squashed the vulnerable tissue. She only had a very short time to open the skull and remove the clot or he would die. She hauled the bundle from the shelf and raced back into Theatre.

She threw the equipment onto the trolley her scrub nurse had hastily prepared. 'Gloves,' she commanded, holding up her hands. 'Quickly.'

'I'll do it.' Suddenly James was there. Still in blues and ungowned, he held up his hands, her nurse gloved him and he swabbed the boy's head with antiseptic, before making an incision directly over the injured part of his skull.

Tessa stumbled back, her knees suddenly weak. 'You've been away so long,' she said faintly. 'I thought you were dead.'

CHAPTER TEN

'JUST busy.' James's eyes were on his work and he didn't look at her. 'I'll do the rest here. Start next door.'

'Yes.' Tessa could hardly walk but she went.

The case next door needed exploratory abdominal surgery. An older man with a long, white beard, his injuries were similar to the women she'd operated on earlier, and the procedure was essentially the same. Axel came in twice during the operation to check his nurse's anaesthetic and he told her that the boy was still alive.

'Huge clot,' he said quickly. 'Fractured skull. He's breathing but, of course, we won't know until later how he is.'

James came to see her as she was closing. 'There's another amputation needed next door—he's stable so it's not an emergency. Do you want to do that while I cover the abdomen that's coming in here?'

Before she could answer Helena shoved open the door. 'Massive chest wounds,' she cried. 'James. . .?'

'Coming.'

He raced after her, leaving Tessa to perform the next abdominal operation. By the time she finished it was late morning. She was hot and tired and bloody, and she gratefully took the tea which one of the aides had brought for her, before pushing open the door to James's theatre to see what he was doing.

When he'd returned from the emergency in triage he'd looked briefly over her shoulder, told her she was doing fine and had gone and done the amputation himself.

Now he'd almost finished performing open chest surgery on another man who'd presented with chest wounds. She watched him carefully insert a wide drain into the space between the lung and its torn lining, then suture

147

the viable remaining muscle into place around it to seal the space closed.

The drain would remove the air and blood from inside the chest, allowing the lung to heal and reinflate.

'What happened to the other chest wound?'

'Didn't make it.' James's voice was grim. 'They got his aorta. God knows how he even made it here.'

He folded the skin closed but didn't suture it, then split a bundle of gauze and folded it to cover the defect and enclose the drain which Axel had inserted into a bottle of water to stop air being sucked back into the chest.

James said, 'Much waiting?'

'Three for wound surgery.' She finished her tea. 'I'll make a start.'

They finished around mid-afternoon. Then she and the other two doctors, plus Mohammed and Helena and Monique, did a complete round, seeing every patient. It took almost four hours. Overnight they'd had thirty-two admissions, had operated on twenty-four and had had three deaths after arrival at hospital.

There were patients in all the beds, on mattresses between the beds and in Outpatients. It was noisy and crowded and hot but there was, at least, a sense that things were under control. Everyone had been assessed and stabilised. There'd been no sounds of guns or rockets since dawn, which meant that by now they'd probably seen their last casualty for the moment.

'Twenty-six dead so far,' said Mohammed. 'They may be finding more in the wreckage, however.' The attacks had devastated the village. Many of those who'd escaped injury had seen their homes destroyed.

'None of this makes sense,' James said quietly, his despair echoing her own feelings. 'It's not a proper war—there's no front line or clearly demarcated territories. These people are civilians, not soldiers.'

'This is Sadakh,' she answered. 'This is how it is here.'

'It's insane.'

'Yes.'

They were going back alone to see the boy whose brain James had operated on earlier. Although still unconscious, he was nevertheless stable and his observations were normal. They hadn't had time to linger on the main round. 'What are his chances?' asked Tessa.

'Not the best.' James shone a torch into each of his eyes. 'We were quick—that's probably the only thing in his favour. The blood clot was massive.'

The nurse looking after him told Tessa that no family had come. 'Perhaps they have died?' she suggested.

'Perhaps.' Tessa looked down at him sadly. He was thin and pale, his shaved head was bruised and scarred below his bandages and his legs and arms were splinted and bandaged—he didn't inspire a lot of hope. And, without family, how would he go in this world even if he did recover?

But she straightened, telling herself she'd been surprised before.

She instructed the nurse to call her if he woke. 'And see if any of the other visitors recognise him,' she added. 'Perhaps his family don't realise he made it to the hospital.'

She went with James back to the mess to join the others and take her place in the queue for a shower. Later, scrubbed clean, she felt more human. She called a staff meeting and while she was waiting for everyone to arrive Mohammed gave her tea and told her about the attack.

'They have been waiting for this,' he told her. 'Of course it is retaliation for the last bombing. Revenge.'

'It is so hard to understand,' Helena said wearily. 'Don't they realise this will just make it all worse?'

'Let's keep this to the practicalities.' Most people were there now and Tessa knew the uselessness of trying to rationalise the violence here. She sat at the table, pen and paper in hand, waiting for them to join her. 'How are we for blood?'

She saw James's head come up, saw the narrowing of his eyes and knew what he wanted to say—what he wanted to forbid—but Mohammed spoke first.

'We've used much of our stored supplies,' he announced, not surprising anyone, 'but we've already begun restocking from donations during the night and today.'

'Saline and dextrose?'

'Plenty.' He nodded. 'The delivery yesterday was very fortunate.'

'How about the lab?'

'They are managing,' he said with reasonable confidence. 'A few small problems with two cross-matchings but otherwise no difficulties.'

Tessa nodded her thanks. 'Surgical supplies?'

'The same,' said Monique. 'No big shortages. Most of last night's equipment is ready to go again.'

'Helena, how about triage?'

'Shortage of splints,' said Helena. 'We have had to use covered metal, bound cardboard and wooden sticks this morning to save the real ones for use in Theatre. James might have some comments.'

James nodded. 'I'd like to equip the Jeep more fully—both Jeeps, if Mohammed's cousin can be persuaded to let us use his. Today, with a few units of blood, some basic surgical equipment and some anaesthetic, there were two other casualties we might have been able to get here in good enough shape for them to survive.'

'It's not usual for a doctor to travel to the scene,' Tessa countered. 'Not while there's still shelling. That was very dangerous. I don't think we should use what happened today as a precedent.'

But Axel supported James. 'People were arriving quickly and already partially resuscitated,' he said. 'That reduces our operative mortality considerably.'

'It's too risky,' she protested.

'We saved lives.' James frowned at her. 'I'm sure of it.'

'We can't afford to lose staff,' Tessa argued, although he was right. 'You both could have been killed.'

'Neither of us is injured,' Mohammed interjected. 'Tessa, you must see that this is part of our job. Remember in the beginning when you started here you were operating sometimes right in the middle of the fighting. Whatever has changed now?'

'If anybody goes next time it should be me,' Tessa said flatly, her determined gaze clashing with James's. 'James, your skills are of more use here in the theatre. I'll organise an emergency box with supplies for the Jeep, and I will go with a driver.'

She saw James stiffen, but the others seemed to agree with her assessment. Even Mohammed was nodding. 'But only if there is trouble in the villages,' he added. 'If there are problems in the town I believe it is quicker for them to come to us.'

'Settled, then.' Not looking at James but sensing his irritation that he'd been outmanoeuvred, Tessa made a meaningless line on her list. 'Khan, how about beds?'

'Totally full,' he said, 'but we have still more mattresses. However, we should not take admissions that are not emergencies.'

'And water?'

'No problems,' he told her. 'There will be enough. And the village is well supplied and the source is clean. The risk of cholera remains low, I believe.'

'Good.' She pushed the paper away from her. 'That seems to be it. I'll take first call from now on until further notice, Axel, you're second and, James, you can be third. There's no reason to be confident there won't be more trouble tonight so we should try and get some rest before dark.'

She left and started to walk towards the ward block, wanting to take another look around.

James followed her. 'It should be me who goes with the Jeep,' he said tightly. 'Without you, this hospital wouldn't even exist. They can't lose you.'

'Nor you,' she retorted.

'I won't let you deliberately put yourself in danger,' he ground out.

Tessa stopped and spun towards him. 'So you admit it.'

'It was necessary.'

'I thought you were both dead.'

'We weren't.'

Her gaze clashed with the blue-grey depths of his. 'James, you can't imagine how I felt.'

'I can imagine.' His face was hard, uncompromising. 'It's exactly the same as I'll feel if you go next time.'

Tessa turned away and started walking quickly. 'There's no point in arguing about this.'

'And you can't give blood again,' he said, catching her easily. 'It's too soon.'

'Mohammed told me you already have,' she countered. 'Technically, that's too soon, too.'

'Only technically.' He caught at her hand and inspected her colour, although she tried to tug it free. 'You're still far too pale. What's your haemoglobin after last time?'

'Haven't checked it.' She glared at him. 'James, stop this,' she warned. 'Stop challenging me. I'm in charge here.'

'It's not a dictatorship,' he countered, unmoved, 'and you've never been a dictator. What's going on, Tessa? What's wrong?'

They were in the corridor now. It was noisy and smelt of blood and antiseptic, and there were people sitting on the floor, holding their infusions high on sticks. She looked around helplessly. 'You have to ask?' she said in wonder. 'All this and you have to ask?'

'Yes.' His mouth tightened. 'This began before the bombing.'

Her head came up and she stared at him, startled by his astuteness. 'I. . . It's Richard,' she said baldly. 'He wants a divorce.'

James's expression stiffened. He took her arm and

guided her into the supply room, shutting the door behind them. 'Tell me.'

She sank onto a carton with her head in her hands and explained everything. 'But she's so young,' she said finally, taking the folded photo from the pocket of her jeans to show him. 'Look. She's not old enough to understand what she's getting into but I can't say anything to her. It isn't fair to either of them and he might have changed.'

She met his doubtful look defensively. 'People do, James. She's young, very beautiful. She could have changed him.'

'She looks like you,' he said quietly. 'The way you used to with your hair long.'

Tessa took back the photo and studied it. There was a superficial resemblance she hadn't noticed before but it was mostly just the hair and the shape of her face. Richard had always preferred blonde women. 'I never had a fringe,' she murmured.

'Second thoughts about wanting him back?'

Tessa blinked. 'No. No, of course not.'

'But you're upset.'

'I don't know what I am.'

'Sad?'

'A little.' She frowned. 'I didn't expect that. I didn't think this would affect me. I feel so. . .selfish.'

'Tessa, Tessa.' James crouched, drawing her unresisting body against his and hugging her. 'Go easy on yourself. You're allowed to have feelings.'

'But I don't understand them,' she protested, her voice muffled against the welcome warmth of him. 'For heaven's sake, I. . . You and I were about to. . .' She burrowed into his shirt. 'You know what we were going to do.'

'Forget that.' But then he drew back, smiling a little, and lifted her hair away from her eyes. 'No, don't forget that,' he added huskily. 'Postpone it.' He stroked the side of her face, a small smile playing at his mouth. 'God knows I'm as guilty as anyone of making demands on you.'

'You don't, though.' His touch was carefully chaste but that hadn't stopped her starting to tingle. 'You help me.'

'Not all the time.' He was watching her mouth and the hands at her back slid to her buttocks, tightened momentarily, hugging her to him, then lifted her away and released her. 'We'd better get out of here.' He opened the door before she had a chance to protest. 'Children's ward?'

'Children's,' she confirmed, sending him a faintly puzzled smile. 'Thank you, James.'

'I haven't done anything.' He swerved around Nazif who was hobbling along the corridor, sparing the boy an encouraging grin. 'Not yet.'

'You listened and that always helps.' She turned to watch Nazif move, impressed. It was less than a week since the rocket attack that had forced her to remove his spleen, and only three days since James had re-explored and closed his wounds, but he was walking now with a determination that suggested they'd be able to discharge him soon.

They continued to walk and she turned back to James, remembering the way he used to listen to her barely formed plans to work in a country like this years ago when they were very junior doctors. Even Richard, who'd been interested in the same future as her, had been bored eventually. But not James. 'You've always listened.'

'Don't be deceived.' He gave her an old-fashioned look. 'I suspect I always had the same motive.'

'I don't think so.' She'd been inexperienced in those days, but not totally naïve—she'd have noticed that. 'I think you're innately kind.'

'You're wrong.' They were inside the ward now, alone at the table at the front, and James's face had hardened abruptly. 'You're wrong, Tessa. I've never been kind.'

'Of course you are.' She smiled. 'Now, what about

this little man?' she asked, looking down at their first patient. 'Do you think we should take his stitches out?'

For a few seconds James studied her but then he shook his head, as if clearing his thoughts, and turned to their patient. 'Sutures out tomorrow at the earliest. I want to look at the wound first.'

'Fine.' She moved on to the next bed.

Khan came to them a few minutes later as she reached the last bed. 'His name is Shinji,' he told them, looking down at the small boy on whom James had performed brain surgery. 'His father has been killed many months ago and his mother has been killed yesterday. Today his grandmother has come to see him.'

Tessa studied the boy's pale face. 'Any movement?'

'A little,' Khan said. 'The eyes haven't opened but he is more awake, I think.'

James crouched to examine him, nodding his agreement as he rose. 'Call me if he wakes during the night,' he instructed.

An uneasy truce stretched over the next few nights, with scattered gunfire the only interruption to the desert silence, but on Sunday night there was another rocket attack, this time on a village several miles to the west of the last attack.

Monique came to wake Tessa, but by the time she got to triage James and Mohammed had already left with the Jeep.

'I told him I was to go,' she protested.

'You knew he would not allow it.' Helena, rolling bandages, barely glanced her way. 'And he was already up. Mohammed had called him to see Fath. He had a fever.'

'But I'm first on call.'

'You can't be that for ever,' Helena answered. 'James overruled you.'

Grateful that neither of the aides helping them spoke English, Tessa said, 'He had no right.'

'Do you think that concerns him?' Finished with the bandages, the nurse threw her a bundle of infusion sets to sort onto the table.

'Well, it should.' Tessa's hands were shaking. She couldn't hear any noise but her heartbeat, but the attack was far away and the quiet didn't mean the shelling had stopped. She collected a bundle of needles and put them close to the infusion sets.

'Wrong size.' Helena clicked her tongue impatiently, bundled the needles back into their box, then steered Tessa away. 'Stop worrying. Go to Theatre. There's nothing you can do.'

'I think I hate him.'

Helena laughed. 'Of course you do,' she said easily. 'I would feel the same about Axel if he did such a thing.' She pushed Tessa in the back. 'Go.'

James came with the first case to Theatre, a boy— probably about eleven or twelve—with chest and abdominal wounds. There was no time for arguments, merely a brief, loaded exchange of looks that warned her he knew of her anger and that she shouldn't expect any compromise from him.

'Cover this,' he said urgently, directing her gloved hand to a bandage he'd folded over a torn part of the child's chest. One drain was already in place, its tubing threaded into a water-filled bottle. James checked the drain, adjusting the tubing slightly. 'I'll scrub. Monique, get him washed and rig up some sterile drapes to cover him. Axel, right lung's completely flat. You won't be able to reinflate until I get a bigger tube in there and close.'

'In hand.' Axel was moving quickly, his normally fair skin flushed. 'Pain relief?'

'Five of morphine thirty minutes ago. I had to give it to get him out. That's his second blood.' As he soaped his hands rapidly James called out instructions for equipment he wanted, sending the aides running as Tessa translated. 'Tessa, you start the abdomen. I'll control the chest, then take over. There's nobody else needing surgery yet.'

'What does it look like?'

'Liver, possibly spleen. I've shoved some packing in there which must be holding them.'

As soon as he returned to the chest Tessa slid along, nodding her thanks for the fresh set of gloves Monique had ready for her.

Using forceps and a scalpel, she gently eased away the edges of the wound and extended it to the base of the patient's breastbone, then stopped, unsure. 'James. . .?'

He leaned across, inspecting the blood-soaked dressings packed inside the abdomen. The surface of the gauze still showed patches of white and no blood rose up, suggesting that he'd managed to stop the bleeding. 'Good.' He nodded towards the liver packing. 'See how you get on, soaking them away.' Dark eyes met hers above their masks. 'All right?'

'Yes.' Without him she would have hesitated, but having him close gave her confidence. She scooped out some loose blood clot. 'Saline?'

'That'll do. Excise what you have to, then huge through and through stitches to pull the liver together and pack.' He returned to the child's chest. 'After this you'll have to think about doing the rest of your exams.'

'Not in this lifetime,' she murmured, taking the large syringe of saline Monique passed her to begin dampening the dressings. Taking the rest of the surgical fellowship exams would mean returning to Britain.

Once the gauze was saturated she lifted it free and then, with James intermittently checking her progress and advising, she carefully lifted away the dying fragment that had been torn away from the main body of the liver.

He joined her as she finished stitching the raw edge. 'We'll pack and leave,' he said firmly, holding up his hands for fresh gloves from Monique and signalling for Tessa to swap sides with him. 'Axel?'

'Holding.' The anaesthetist hadn't had time even to pick up his novel, and he spared them only a brief glance as he connected another unit of blood. 'Tessa, next visit to your wonderful London, a reliable oximeter, please.'

'Top of my list.' An oximeter provided a measure of the amount of oxygen in a patient's blood and Axel had struggled with the very old one they had for far too long now. A replacement was her next planned major purchase.

Tessa suctioned away the blood and saline while James cleared the packing he'd laid on the left side of the abdomen. She assisted him to expose the spleen. 'Taking it out?'

'No choice.' James reached for a bundle of artery forceps. 'It's a mess. We're taking the spleen, Axel. Then some bowel as well.'

'Of course.' Axel rolled his eyes. 'Any organ still intact in this child?'

'Heart.' James began clamping. 'I hope.'

Tessa assisted him to remove the spleen then she left him to finish while she went to check the remainder of the casualties.

There were three other admissions, aside from the boy—his mother and two cousins, all with relatively minor injuries that Mohammed and Helena had treated.

Helena took Tessa to see the mother. Despite both arms being in slings, she struggled out of bed as they approached.

'My son?' she cried, her face damp with tears. 'How is my son?'

Tessa explained about the surgery, about how James was doing everything he could.

'It is in God's hands,' proclaimed the weeping woman. 'Your doctor is our hero. He went amongst everything to find my son. Things were still falling. He spared no thought for his own life.'

'I'll come back when I have news,' Tessa said abruptly, not wanting to hear about that.

One of the nurses called her to see a newly born baby at the other end of the ward, and by the time she got back to Theatre it was light and they were finishing. 'He's stable,' James told her, helping Axel to lift their patient onto a clean trolley. The one they'd been working on was blood-stained. 'Now all we need is a decent paediatric ICU.'

'With an arterial line,' agreed Axel, dreaming the impossible—controlling the child's head and nodding approval as Mohammed clamped off the chest drains while they transported.

'How about a clean bed and a private nurse?' Tessa said brightly.

'Marvellous.' James, still gowned, leaned across the bed and kissed her. 'Have I told you yet how gorgeous you look this morning?'

'Don't think I've forgotten you took the Jeep,' she countered and pulled back abruptly, her flush deepening as she noted the obvious amusement of everyone in the theatre. Everyone except Monique, whom she saw turn abruptly away.

'You are always sleeping through the emergencies.' Axel waved his hand at Tessa dismissively as they wheeled the trolley out. 'Be awake more often.'

'Thanks, Monique,' she said, when she and the nurse were left alone. 'You did a good job there.'

'I am very good always.' The younger woman was sniffing as she sorted her instruments. 'I am thinking I would like to leave.' She looked directly at Tessa. 'I should like to go to America to work. Richard has said he would be able to find me a job there if I wanted.'

Tessa closed her eyes briefly and said gently, 'Richard is getting married again.'

'No.' Monique's face began to crumple. 'No. I don't believe you. It's impossible.'

'I'm sorry.' Tessa pushed the trolley away so she could hug her. She patted her trembling shoulders and let her weep. 'I'm sorry, Monique.'

'It isn't fair,' she wailed.

James appeared in the doorway, his eyebrows rising when he saw them, and Tessa shook her head to wave him away. 'I know he wasn't fair,' she said softly.

Slowly Monique lifted her head. 'You could give me James,' she said croakily, blinking her reddened eyes at Tessa. 'That might help me.'

'You can't "give" people,' Tessa chided. 'James does what he wants to do.'

Monique's breath heaved. 'But if you tell him you don't want him—if you sent him away—'

'No.' Now that the sobs had stopped Tessa let her arms drop. 'No, Monique. I'm not going to do that. Not with James.'

'Then I want to leave.' Monique straightened her shoulders. 'I think I will leave, please.'

'If that's what you want then of course.' Tessa studied her sadly. 'But don't tell me now—leave it a few days. You're upset now. Wait until you're calmer.'

Monique stepped back, using her sleeve to wipe her face. 'Yes.' She lifted her head. 'I will speak with James first.'

'You have to make your own decision,' Tessa said carefully, worried by that.

'I know.' Monique returned to her trolley. 'I will tell you.'

Deciding that there was nothing to be gained by more discussion, Tessa walked across to the mess.

James and Axel were there but Axel left almost immediately to go and check on their newest patient. James held out his arms and when she went to him he hugged her. 'They deserved each other,' he said quietly, proving he'd overheard more of her talk with the nurse than she'd hoped.

She closed her eyes, but her silence was enough for him and his arms tightened.

'Oh, Tessa.' He rocked her gently and kissed her hair. 'Richard's insane—nothing else makes sense.'

Burrowed into the comforting, strong warmth of him with her face pressed to the opening in his shirt, Tessa decided that was the nicest thing anyone had ever said to her. She touched his chest with her mouth, feeling him tense as the intensity of their embrace changed. 'James. . .?'

But he released her abruptly and unravelled her arms so he could step free. 'I need a shower,' he said roughly, turning away from her so she couldn't see his expression. 'How about we meet in Children's in an hour?'

'OK.' She frowned her puzzlement but he was gone before she framed the words to question him.

The next days were busy for all of them. James covered the theatre work, completing and closing the wounds from the second major rocket attack, while Tessa looked after the wards and clinics and helped him when she could.

To their joy Shinji woke, and although he had no memory of the attack that had killed his mother there were no signs of disabling brain damage. And the child with the terrible chest and abdominal wounds whose liver she had repaired seemed equally determined to recover.

At least two or three emergency admissions each night interrupted their sleep and kept them busy until morning again, but as the attacks were on the town itself no hospital staff had to leave the hospital to retrieve the casualties who arrived instead in battered vehicles and on the backs of donkey-drawn wagons.

Thursday night brought its characteristic calm and Friday was quiet. James was in the mess when she got up and they went to the wards together, Tessa munching her peanut-butter-spread toast as they walked.

He eyed her breakfast. 'You must be getting low.'

'Not even close,' she said cheerfully. 'Still on the third jar.'

'And seven to go.' He smiled. 'Amazing.'

'There must be worse vices,' she countered, meeting

his gently amused gaze meaningfully. 'Not that I'd know.'

'Not that you would.' His hand on the small of her back guided her into the building and made her tingle. 'Be grateful for small mercies, Tessa Mathesson.'

But she wasn't grateful, she reflected irritably as they strode towards the men's ward. Not grateful at all. Which made it doubly ironic that James appeared to have lost interest in her. The past few days had been busy and they were both tired but the night before had been quiet, yet he'd turned down her pointed invitation for an evening stroll.

Helena joined them as they finished seeing their male patients, coming with them to Women's and Children's.

Twins had been born overnight and, although Tessa had been woken during the night to supervise the delivery, she left the others for a few minutes once they'd finished on the ward so she could examine the babies and their young mother again to make sure there were no problems that needed her attention.

Aside from their low birth weights, both girls seemed fine. Although their mother was tired she was well, and after congratulating Karima again on her skilled delivery Tessa crossed back to the mess.

As she reached the door she almost collided with Monique. The nurse who was clad only in a thin towel, her face and neck pink and blotchy, stormed out, not even looking at her.

'Monique. . .?' Tessa tried to catch her arm as she swung past. Since their talk in the operating theatre Monique had said no more about leaving but Tessa had sensed her unhappiness and it had been worrying her. 'Are you all right?'

The younger woman whirled to face her. 'Leave me,' she shouted, clutching at the edges of her towel with her free hand. 'I hate you,' she snarled. 'You always want everything—all the men.'

Tessa paled. Holding the shaking girl's arm, she said

firmly, 'No one hates anyone, Monique. Not here. You know that. What's wrong? What's happened?'

'Don't bother with her.' Suddenly Helena was there. She said something very fast in Dutch which Tessa didn't understand, and Monique shouted back, then turned and ran off towards her room, sobbing.

'What's going on?' Tessa turned to Helena, her eyes wide. 'Tell me.'

Helena said something that sounded vicious in Dutch. 'With Richard I pretend I see nothing for your sake,' she added in English. 'With James, I ignore—he can handle her. But with Axel. . .?' Her face was dark with fury. 'With Axel I say stop. With Axel I tell her some facts she doesn't like.'

Tessa's head whirled. 'James?' she said faintly. 'Axel?'

'Nothing has happened.' Axel, wearing bright pink pyjama pants and nothing else, emerged from the room. 'She comes to my room that silly girl. Naked. That is all.'

Helena said something else in Dutch.

'And you, my beautiful Dutch Amazonian.' Axel was laughing as he tugged the furious Helena into his arms. 'You come to my rescue. I cannot live without you. You must marry me—marry me today.'

'We don't have a celebrant,' said Tessa sensibly, still shaking as Helena dissolved into laughing tears.

'Then we take our vows before you,' said Axel, kissing his bride-to-be. 'Before the world. Before the sky.' He danced Helena around. 'James can be best man.'

'James hasn't got a suit,' said James, emerging from the mess to watch them dance.

'Then we have to wait,' said Axel, scooping Helena up into his arms. He growled. 'But we start the honeymoon this minute.'

Tessa laughed as the pair hurried along the corridor to Axel's room, her emotions still swinging wildly as she turned back to James. 'What happened?'

He lifted one broad shoulder. 'Helena took Axel tea

in bed and then she chased the pair of them out here.
The rest you know.'

She followed him into the mess. 'I should go and
talk to her.'

'No.' James sprawled in the easy chair, regarding her
broodingly. 'Leave her. She's an adult, even if it suits
her to play the child with you. Give her some time. Let
her make the decisions she needs to make.'

But Tessa wasn't sure that solitude would help her do
that. Monique had never been strong on insight—she
needed support. But acknowledging that he was probably
right about Monique needing time at present, she stayed.
She poured them both tea. 'Helena mentioned you,' she
said quietly. 'Did Monique do the same to you?'

'Only once.' James took the tea and swung his leg over
the arm of the chair, not appearing especially concerned.
'Not again.'

But Tessa's mouth had dropped open. 'Was she. . .
naked?'

'Yes.' He tilted his head, his eyes narrowing. 'Don't
ask her to stay, Tessa. It isn't good for her any more.
She's not strong enough. She should go back to
Europe.'

'She's already mentioned wanting to leave.' Tessa
sank onto the seat beside him, numbly sipping her drink.
'Did she speak to you?'

'I don't think I told her what she wanted to hear.'

'I don't think she knows what that is.' Tessa sighed.
'I thought Richard was entirely to blame with Monique.
The fact that she might have given him some encourage-
ment never occurred to me. He never told me even when
I was so angry with him. He just went. I thought. . .
I thought he'd finally realised he'd done something
rather awful.'

'It must have been time for him to go.'

'It was. I think he'd wanted to leave for ages.
Seems funny. I can't imagine ever actually choosing
to leave.'

'Richard and Monique have very different personalities to you.'

'Oh, James.' And soon he would be leaving, too. Tessa shook her head. 'What a mess this all is.'

'It is a bit.' He lowered his cup to the floor and took her hand. 'Don't worry about her. She can look after herself. More, I suspect,' he said gently, drawing her onto his lap, 'than you.'

'I'm fine.'

'Hmm.' He sounded doubtful, the finger that played at her mouth playfully teasing. 'You're so gentle,' he said softly, nuzzling her forehead. 'We all take advantage of you.'

'I don't care.' She snuggled closer, loving the feeling of being close to him after what seemed like weeks of him holding her away. 'Why have you been avoiding me?'

'Because you're irresistible.' He laughed, then captured the mouth that opened to bite him, his murmur of approval at her response changing to a growl as she twisted to straddle him.

'Tessa. . .?'

'Yes, James.' Tessa's fingers curled in the strong warmth of his hair, holding him to her. 'I've missed you.'

'I've been here.' His mouth lowered to her throat and he licked the pulse that beat frantically beneath her skin.

'Not properly.'

'As properly as I could.' He bit her earlobe. 'As properly as was good for you.'

She tilted her head back, her mouth opening with delight at his touch. 'Please. . .?'

'Please, what?' His hand slid to cup her breast, sending showers of pinpricks scattering over her skin. 'Please, this?'

'Yes.' She gasped when his hands shifted and curled around her thighs to urge her closer to him.

'Ah, Tessa.' James buried his face in her throat again, his hands sliding beneath her shirt to roam restlessly across her back. 'You tempt me.'

'I think that's what I want to do.' She kissed him, opened her mouth on his, tasted him. She was nervous suddenly, but her desire was greater. 'Let's go to bed.'

CHAPTER ELEVEN

James stilled. 'Tessa. . .?'

'I'm sure.' She regarded him steadily. 'I'm not going to change my mind again. I promise.'

'I pressured you.'

'Not this time. Now I'm deciding myself. Really. Please.'

'Then, yes.' He hugged her hard, then lifted her, carrying her easily to his room as she rained tiny kisses across his face. He tumbled her onto the bed and followed her.

The warm afternoon breeze stirred across her heated skin from the shutters he'd left open to the desert, and she arched in pleasure as he worked his way down her body, baring her.

'Oh, no, stop.' Suddenly she wriggled free and rolled from the bed, pulling her shirt together where he'd parted it. 'Stop. Have you got a pen?'

'Pen?' James looked bemused. He struggled up. 'Tessa. . .?'

'Just a pen.' Tessa whirled around, looking. She'd left hers on a ward somewhere and she knew there were none in her room. 'A pen. Just a pen.'

'Here.' He handed her a black ballpoint. 'Where are you going?'

'I'll be back.' She pulled the door shut and ran to her room. She opened her drawer and hauled out the envelope, almost tearing the documents in her haste to get at them. Hurriedly she flicked through them, initialling each page before scrawling her signature and the date on the last one.

Then, after shoving the whole lot carelessly back into the drawer, she ran to James. The gesture had been symbolic, she acknowledged. She couldn't post the papers until the next plane arrived but, still, she felt that she'd done the right thing.

'I'm back.' He was sitting on the edge of the bed and she hesitated inside the door. 'I'm out of practice at this,' she said faintly, nervous again without the reassurance of his touch.

He stilled. 'Come here.'

She went into his arms, tipped him back and let him gather her against him. 'Tell me if I do something wrong.'

'You never could.' His voice was rough-edged, husky against the skin of her throat. 'Besides, I want to do everything.' He pulled her shirt apart again and lowered his mouth to her flesh. He suckled her breast while his determined hands freed her jeans. 'You taste delicious. Peanut butter sundae.'

She laughed as he rolled her beneath him, tugging off the last of her clothes. 'I haven't had any today,' she told him. 'Perhaps we should eat. . .?'

'Later.' His grin was lazy but he held her down easily, capturing her wrist in one strong hand and forcing her to lie back. 'This first,' he said deeply, his mouth lowering to the quivering tightness of her stomach. 'This first.'

Later, when she was sweat-soaked and exhausted, drowsy with delight, he twisted her onto her side so she faced away then pulled her back against him, one hand lazily drawing patterns against her stomach as they lay watching the sky turn pink.

'I love you,' she whispered. 'You must know that already.'

'God, Tessa.' His voice at her neck rasped against her skin and that hand at her stomach stilled. 'No. That wasn't meant to happen.'

'I know.' Filled with joy and yet at the same time utterly sad, she sighed. 'I sort of thought it would, though,' she admitted quietly, 'but it doesn't matter.'

'Don't.' He kissed the top of her head. 'Don't, Tessa. Go to sleep.'

'Yes.' Obediently she closed her eyes. 'I don't want you to worry,' she whispered. 'It really doesn't matter.'

No one disturbed them for dinner and they woke hungry at midnight, ate leftover rice, then made love until they fell asleep in each other's arms.

The next day they ate breakfast with the others. Axel and Helena were preoccupied with each other but Monique's resentful stare suggested that she understood what had been going on.

'Please request an aeroplane,' she said to Tessa when they went together across to the wards. 'I am missing my family. I should like to go home.'

'Of course.' Tessa steered the nurse into her office. 'Monique, you're upset and obviously homesick, and it's a little frightening here at the moment. Everybody understands how you're feeling—we've all been through this. Please don't feel bad about what's happened.'

'I do not feel bad,' the nurse answered stiffly. 'Helena is always jealous, that is her problem. She doesn't understand that Axel is not content with her.' She pushed back her hair. 'I am tired of working with her,' she declared.

Tessa sighed and decided there was little to be gained by pushing the issue. 'It may take some time to organise your flight.'

'When is it possible, please?'

'I'll try today.' Tessa frowned. 'Of course, you don't have to worry about your contract—I'll explain to the agency that I'm releasing you.'

Monique sniffed. 'I will expect payment for this full three months. I would not be leaving if it were not for Helena.'

'I'll see what I can do.' Tessa sighed again, wondering how she was going to talk the agency into that. Wishing that she had money of her own which she could give the nurse to avoid awkward questions was fruitless, though. Every scrap of income she'd accumulated in the past had been spent on this hospital.

'And I shall be working in Theatre until I leave,' Monique added as she opened the door. 'Please tell Helena. I do not want more arguments.'

'We appreciate the help,' Tessa said gently, her shoulders loosening when the door closed. Fervently hoping that their new nurse appointment—if he had passed the interview—would be more amenable, she went to find Mohammed to ask him what supplies he needed. They may as well take advantage of Monique's flight to try and obtain an early delivery.

There were more casualties that night and Helena, coming to fetch them, discovered that Tessa was sharing James's bed. Her smile, as they dashed across to triage together—James was already ahead of them on his way to Theatre—was approving. 'Two honeymoons,' she declared happily.

'Not exactly.' Tessa avoided her knowing eyes, knowing she'd have need enough of Helena's sympathy when James left. 'Many injuries?'

'Two or three. Perhaps more coming.'

There were several more, and Tessa went to Theatre to help. Helena brought in her second case, a pale, unconscious child, calling to her urgently as she scrubbed to tell her about the girl. 'Abdominal injuries,' she told her quickly, 'but I can't hold the blood pressure.' A bag of blood and one of saline were already infusing. 'James is operating on another child next door; he'll come when he can. Do you want to start?'

Tessa decided she had little choice. The child's injuries looked massive, but if she didn't do anything immediately she'd die.

But, shortly into the case, Tessa had to call for his help. The girl's abdomen had been shredded by shrapnel, the peritoneum filled with blood and bowel debris that continued to well up too fast for her suction tube to cope, despite her every effort to control it. 'I can't stop it,' she said urgently, wrapping the injured bowel in damp gauze to try and contain its contents. 'It's coming from everywhere.'

'Losing blood pressure.' The anaesthetic nurse was yelling for Axel to come. 'Pulse one-seventy-six.'

'Liver, spleen, pancreas, gut, probably her kidneys as well,' James said quickly beside her, assessing the damage as she frantically suctioned blood to try and clear a view for him. 'Forget it, Tessa. No chance.'

'She's alive.'

'Only technically.' Axel had come running. 'Ventricular fibrillation on the monitor. Shall I shock?'

'No.'

'Yes.' Tessa spoke at the same time as James.

But Axel was watching James and he didn't move. 'Straight line,' he said quietly, after a few fraught seconds. 'That's it. Finished.'

And James and Axel rushed back to their own case, leaving her theatre suddenly quiet. Tessa's shoulders sagged and her eyes ached as she gently sutured her little patient's abdomen closed, before allowing her to be carried away.

A middle-aged woman with left leg injuries replaced the child who'd died on her table, and Tessa worked mechanically to explore and clean her wounds.

They finished operating shortly after sunrise. She and Axel and James did their usual post-theatre ward round and then James made her tea and toast, thickly spread with peanut butter, in the mess.

He sat opposite. 'Do you want to talk about it?'

'No.' She concentrated on her breakfast. 'She was seven years old.'

'I've been surprised,' he said quietly, 'how few deaths we've seen here. Despite the conditions, this hospital does very good work.'

'If you'd been operating from the start could you have saved her?'

'No.' There wasn't any doubt on his face or in his voice. 'Not here. Possibly not even in the best unit in

London. A good team might have got her through the surgery but not necessarily the sepsis or organ failure afterwards.'

'Should I have even started?'

'It's not easy not to,' he replied carefully. 'I might not have but, then, you're not as experienced.'

That reminded her that when he left she'd be operating alone again. 'I'll miss you.'

'I'm not going yet.' Silently he stood and took her hand and took her to his bed. He made love to her with a gentle tenderness that made her weep, and then he bathed away her tears under the shower.

Towards sunset they walked about a mile away from the hospital in the direction of the airport where they would have a clear view of the mountains for the rising of the full moon between them. It was her favourite place from which to watch it and she tried to come each month if she could, but James was the first person who'd ever been interested enough to walk with her.

They sat on the road—Tessa between his legs with her head against his warm chest and his arms around her—to wait, both quiet.

Because of the height of the mountains it took time for the moon to appear and she caught her breath at the first stunning glimpse of it as it began to light the darkened sky, throwing the huge black shadows of the peaks into stark silhouette.

Huge and orange, the moon rose swiftly, shrinking and becoming paler as it soared into clear sky. 'Isn't it amazing?' she whispered, overawed as always.

'Beautiful.' James nuzzled her forehead, his eyes on the sky. 'How long have you been coming here?'

'Practically every month since I arrived.' The moon was high now and she leaned back in his arms, closing her eyes. 'It still seems incredible.'

James lay back on the road, taking her with him and twisting her so that she lay above him. His hand twined in her hair and he lowered her mouth to his. When the kiss finished he stroked her hair. 'Are you too cold?'

'Too warm.' Her urgent fingers fumbled with the buttons of her shirt. 'Help me.'

'Yes.' He brushed her hands aside, opened her clothing and parted her thighs so that she sat across him. 'You're trembling.'

She kissed him, moved on him urgently, no longer nervous with him. 'Now, James.'

At dinner Mohammed told her he'd heard from the capital that an aeroplane would come within the next three days, possibly even on the following one.

'At last.' The arrangement had been made with a speed that astonished Tessa but Monique sounded aggrieved, as if she'd been waiting months instead of only a few days. The nurse had finished her meal and she pushed her plate away and moved from the table. 'I will pack.'

Helena rolled her eyes as Monique left but to Tessa's relief said nothing. The situation was bad enough, without them discussing it.

James said, 'Does that give us enough time to get supplies organised?'

'Probably not.' Tessa looked doubtfully at Mohammed who shrugged, and she decided that at this stage it was more important to get Monique out. 'We'll be able to send our mail, but that's possibly all.'

Helena was pouring tea for them all when there was shouting from the hospital and Karima came running across. 'Come, please,' she said, gesturing. 'A boy. He is shot.' She looked helplessly at Tessa. 'His brother brought him. We don't know. . .?'

They all ran across, Tessa translating for James. When they reached Theatre she froze, understanding the reason for Karima's uncertainty. A young soldier, still in uniform, lay on a stretcher, groaning. Blood was seeping from his abdomen and staining his torn shirt.

No one had inserted any lines yet, and James went for a cannula, shouting instructions to the nurses. 'Blood,' he said urgently. 'What the hell's going on? He's here now—we have to treat him. Someone get me blood.'

His certainty jolted her, and she stared at the boy's pale, contorted face. 'It might have been an accident,' she said tightly. 'Perhaps his brother shot him?' Then, knowing what they were doing wasn't careful or wise but speaking from a heart that loved James for what he was doing she said, 'James is right. We can't just let him die.'

There were no arguments, only one brief, concerned look from Helena as her words sent everyone spiralling wordlessly into action. Within minutes Axel had administered pain relief and an anaesthetic and their patient was being lifted onto an operating trolley and moved into Theatre.

'I am sorry.' Karima touched her arm briefly, gesturing for her to come. 'There is another.'

Tessa murmured an explanation to James so he'd understand why she wasn't scrubbing to assist him and went with the nurse.

It was the boy's brother. He was also in uniform and he'd also been shot, but the bullets had merely brushed his skin, leaving a superficial wound. He offered no explanation and she didn't ask for one, knowing that by now it was too late to prevent any repercussions if there were to be any.

It was the sort of injury the nurses would normally have dealt with independently but Tessa wouldn't let them assist. She cleansed the wound herself, gave him a tetanus inoculation and antibiotics.

'From now, nothing has changed,' she told him quietly, knowing he'd understand. 'You must not come again. Go. You are safer away from here. Warn your colleagues.'

He clasped her hands briefly, murmuring thanks, and left.

James came to see her in her office after Theatre. 'He's alive,' he said grimly, 'but critical. What's going to happen?'

'I don't know.' She hid her terror. They'd never treated military casualties at the hospital. It was an agreement they'd made with all sides to prevent themselves becoming embroiled in the conflict. She didn't know how the opposition militia would react but she had her suspicions, suspicions she wasn't going to share with him.

'Perhaps nothing will happen,' she said huskily. 'Perhaps no one will find out.'

'I couldn't let him die in front of us.'

'I know.' She saw his frustration and shared it, but there was nothing she could do.

'If anything happens it was my decision to treat him,' he said quietly. 'Let me talk to them. I'll go to see them if it's necessary. Try to explain.'

Tessa couldn't look at him. They wouldn't be looking for explanations. Without saying anything, she nodded.

The soldiers came early next morning.

For the first time in more than a year Tessa hadn't been able to sleep. She'd made gentle, lingering love with James, staying quiet in his arms until his breathing steadied, then crept to her office.

When she heard the noise she knew who it would be and went running.

There were four of them. Heavily armed. They wore neat blue uniforms where the boys earlier had worn ragged khaki.

Two aides were there, and a nurse, cowering as they confronted the men. Tessa ordered her staff out of the way, pushing them into the children's ward when they hesitated.

The tallest of the group, the man whom she assumed was in charge, barked his complaint, and she nodded acknowledgement that they'd treated the boys.

'I am deeply sorry,' she said quietly. 'I have made a mistake. Please do not blame the hospital.'

They wanted to be taken to the soldier but she denied them that. And she'd been careful to make sure that all traces of his militia group had been removed, destroyed.

Her denial angered them. 'Are you asking us to kill all of your patients until we find him?' the leader demanded.

She stood her ground. 'I am asking your forgiveness.'

'There must be retribution.'

Tessa understood that. That was the way Sadakh society worked and she'd prepared herself for that. 'He was wounded here,' she said quietly, indicating her abdomen.

The man nodded. If he was surprised by her words he didn't show it. 'It is fair.'

He nodded to the smaller man at his side who lifted his weapon and shot her.

CHAPTER TWELVE

TESSA had expected to die, or at least lose consciousness, but she didn't.

There was burning pain that rapidly dulled, then a liquid spreading pain in her abdomen through to her back—but she was awake. She held her hand over her wound to stem the bleeding as she watched the soldiers calmly leave. Then the nurses were around her and there was running and noise and screaming.

Suddenly James was there and his eyes were brilliant, burning blue and she flinched from the accusation she read in them while he shouted and touched her face. And then he was lifting her with Axel's help, and there were needles and darkness and blessed relief.

When she woke from the anaesthetic James was there. 'I could kill you,' he grated. 'If you weren't already half-dead I swear I would have. How dared you take that for me?'

'Is the boy still all right?'

'He's fine.'

'We did the right thing.' She went back to sleep, smiling.

Helena was there when she woke again. 'He is working,' she said briskly, reading the question in her eyes before her parched throat could voice it. '*Trying* to work. Madwoman.'

'I had no choice,' she whispered.

'He's sending you to London.'

'No!' Her voice was cracked and hoarse as she tried to lift herself up, but Helena's hand at her chest pushed her back.

'If you fight he will sedate you,' she said unsympa-

177

thetically. 'Monique is to be your private nurse for the journey. No more than you deserve.'

Tessa touched her bandage-swathed abdomen. 'What. . .?'

'You'll live.'

But Helena didn't seem to find the fact especially cheering. She picked up a mug of red liquid and swabbed the parched inside of Tessa's mouth, leaving it fresh and cool and tingling from the antiseptic.

The nurse injected a syringe of clear fluid into the line in Tessa's arm. 'Antibiotics,' she said crisply. 'But time you went back to sleep.'

Later Tessa was dimly aware of being taken in the Jeep and of James holding her hand as they crawled slowly towards the airport. As each jolt sent pain through her back for once she was grateful for Mohammed's slow driving.

She heard the plane land, then saw James inject something into her drip, felt his mouth at her cheek—and then nothing.

Two days later Tessa was sitting up in a freshly made bed in London's Royal Free Hospital. The private ward she'd found herself in was almost at the top of the high-rise hospital and she had a view over Hampstead and the edge of its famous heath. Pretty, she conceded, having made the effort to hobble to the window. But she missed the view from her room in Sadakh.

'You were lucky,' her consultant told her, his terseness suggesting he might have been told she'd brought her injuries on herself. 'James had to take some gut but you're not going to miss it much. No signs of a leak. Try some soup and see how you go.'

'Who's paying for this?' she demanded of the agency's chairman when he brought her orchids, which she hated, and chocolates, which she liked but which he appeared determined to eat.

'Not us,' he said cheerfully, his mouth full of caramel

delight. 'Thank God. Apparently there was a hell of a battle about the evacuation—something about not being able to fly above a certain altitude after your surgery.' He took another chocolate. 'Must have cost a fortune.'

He munched thoughtfully. 'Got a bill this morning from the nurse you had as an escort.' His whistle suggested that it had been a big one. 'Sent that on to the man with the chequebook quick smart.'

'I want to go back.' Tessa struggled into a sitting position, holding her stomach with her hand. She'd been up that morning to shower and take another walk but it was still painful when she put any strain on it. 'I'll be out of here by the end of the week. Two weeks to get my strength back, then out to Sadakh. OK?'

But Rupert, studying the chart which had come with the chocolates to decide his next selection, frowned. 'No can do, Tessa. Sorry. The word is six months' recuperation. Minimum.'

'The word. . .?' She scowled at him. 'Whose word?'

'Just *the* word.' He took more chocolates. 'We're flying in that nurse we wrote to you about this week, along with a locum paediatrician to fill in for you. You're surplus. And you need a holiday. Spend some time with your family.'

'How did you get the paediatrician?'

'Money talks.' Now Rupert had finished all but the toffees he seemed to think the visit was over and he stood, smoothing the creases from his trousers. 'See you, Tessa. Give me a call April some time.'

'Rupert, wait.' She couldn't believe this. 'What money? What do you mean—April? And I'm not surplus—it's *my* hospital. I'm in charge.'

'You've been usurped.' He didn't stop. 'Not before April, Tessa.'

'You can't do this to me,' she shrieked. But he was gone.

*   *   *

It took her six weeks to start feeling anything like fit again. Without a guarantee and letter of support from the agency, the Sadakhi embassy in Paris refused to even consider issuing her another entry visa, and it took another month to bludgeon Rupert into changing his mind.

Five days later she was in a small plane above the hospital.

James and Mohammed came to fetch her. James looked furious. 'I told them six months,' he raged. 'It's barely been three.'

'I missed you too.' Conscious of the pilot and Mohammed watching, she resisted the nearly over-whelming urge to throw herself into his arms and contented herself with a brief handshake which did nothing to dampen her craving for him.

While he strode irritably away to help the others unload Tessa spun around, inhaling the frost-crisp air and mar-velling at the snow-drenched beauty of the mountains behind them—so different from their dusty autumn arid-ness when she'd left. And so majestically impelling after the dull London January she'd escaped.

'Prickles is growing fast,' she told James *en route* to the hospital a short while later. He'd written to her through Rupert, reassuring her that he'd arranged to remain in Sadakh until after her return and inviting her to use his house and car, if she wanted, in London. And, of course, she'd wanted. 'She's living at Monica's now— she got lonely without you.' As she, herself, had, Tessa reflected dryly. She and Prickles had been rather forlorn companions for each other.

'You've lost weight.'

'I'm putting it back on again.' She beamed. 'Mohammed, you're looking especially handsome this morning.'

'A special outfit to honour your return,' he said, smil-ing at her. 'My family have brought it from the capital.'

'They're back?' Tessa was very pleased. 'So the war is quiet?'

'The truce is holding,' James said flatly. 'No major incidents for two months now.'

'A miracle.' He was sitting next to her, and she couldn't stop her hand from drifting to smooth his hair. 'More grey,' she said lightly, teasing a few strands.

'Hardly surprising.' He captured her hand and pressed his mouth to her wrist, anger still sparkling in the blue depths of his eyes. 'If you ever do anything so stupid again I will kill you. Understand?'

Breathlessly mute, Tessa concentrated on the movement of his mouth against her skin. Three months had been too long to be away from him. Even after the pain of her injuries had receded she'd ached, every day, for James.

'Axel?' she asked huskily, her eyes locked with James's. 'Helena and Karima? Little Shinji? All the others?'

'Every one of them fine,' Mohammed said cheerfully when James didn't reply, jolting them with characteristic slowness over a bumpy patch in the road. 'Shinji is completely recovered from his head injury and is living with his brothers and his grandmother. And we are quiet at the moment. We will have a party for your return.'

'I'd like that.'

James pushed up the sleeve of her jumper to reveal the pale underside of her forearm which he proceeded to kiss, making Tessa's head spin. 'Um. . .I visited Monique in Amsterdam,' she said roughly, talking fast to cover her breathlessness. 'She has a good job and a new boyfriend. She seemed happy.'

'That is very good.' Mohammed turned gently into the hospital. 'A boyfriend of her own is what she was always wanting, I think.'

'Yes.' Tessa eased her wrist and then her hand free from James's grip, her face hot and flustered as she climbed carefully out of the Jeep. 'I'm home,' she murmured, looking around at the small cluster of buildings, pleasure at the feeling swelling within her.

'Tessa!' Helena came running from the ward block, her arms outstretched and her face wet with tears of welcome. 'We have missed you so much.' And she caught her up in a hug and there were kisses and then Axel was there, too, his round face split with a huge beam.

'For this glorious day I will prepare my special Finnish chicken Maryland,' he declared.

'What a wonderful welcome.' Tessa hugged him again, laughing, and rolled her eyes apologetically over his shoulder at Helena, James and a stricken-looking Mohammed. 'I can't wait.'

James wouldn't allow her to help unload the Jeep so she went into the mess with Helena for tea while he and Mohammed organised the supplies she'd brought with her. Another load would be coming in a few weeks, bringing the equipment she'd bought with the money from the luncheon Delia Buttrose-Allen had staged for her.

She told Helena about it. 'Only problem is she wants to visit us.' She laughed. 'She's terribly posh. I can't imagine it, but she wants James to do her bunion or some nonsense like that. Apparently, his secretary told her rather grumpily that the only way she'll get him is to come out here.'

'She might be right.' James appeared in the doorway, his face shadowed and his eyes gleaming.

Helena murmured something indistinct, then darted around him and away.

Tessa stood slowly. 'I told her you'd be back in London within a month,' she said huskily. 'I said you'd already stayed longer here than you wanted.'

'Really?' He held out his hand and she walked towards him, let him lead her to his room. 'Interesting.'

'But it's true,' she said faintly, standing rigid as he shut the door behind them, lifted her jumper over her head and calmly began to unbutton her shirt. 'Isn't it?'

James unfastened her jeans, tugging them down until she stepped out of them. 'Not bad,' he said, his finger tracing her scars. 'Considering.'

'I heal well.' She couldn't tear her eyes away from the compelling darkness of his. 'It's only a year since Jean-Paul had to take out my appendix—you can barely make out the scar now.'

James stripped his clothes in a few brief, precise movements, his eyes holding her mesmerised as he backed her slowly to the bed. 'Which room did you use at the house?'

'Yours.' Her mouth was so dry she could barely speak.

'Good.' He drew her forward and lifted her, his mouth playing at hers—making her shiver. 'I imagined you there.'

Tessa twined her legs around his thighs, gripping him as he went forward onto the bed. 'I imagined you there, too.'

'Like this?'

'Every night.' She turned her head slowly into the blankets as his head lowered to her breasts. 'Oh, James.'

Afterwards he held her close, his hand sliding to trace the faintly puckered length of her wound. 'I will never forgive you for this,' he said roughly.

'They would have destroyed the hospital,' she whispered. 'Or killed our patients. I couldn't do anything else. Even if they didn't do those things we'd have become a legitimate target and we couldn't have carried on.'

'It was my responsibility, not yours.' He spun her abruptly and buried his head in her stomach. 'You're not safe to be left alone.'

Tessa curled up, embracing him. 'I missed you so much. How could you send me away?'

'For your good and my sanity.' James groaned. He lifted his head briefly so that she saw his pain then lowered it again, pressing her into the thin foam of the mattress. 'Bloody Rupert,' he raged. 'He knew I wanted you kept in Britain. You can't be strong enough yet for here. He's not getting his bonus.'

'I'm strong,' she insisted, understanding suddenly why Rupert had been so uncharacteristically difficult to persuade. 'This money he kept talking about—that's your money?'

'My money, your money—who cares?' He kissed her, a tender, hungry, loving kiss. 'I'm in charge now, Tessa. Did he tell you that?'

Tessa stiffened, the languid softness of her limbs evaporating abruptly. 'He told me I'd been usurped,' she said carefully, 'but I ignored him as usual.'

'Big mistake.' He looked at her, his eyes dark. 'I pulled strings.'

'You mean you bribed him.' She struggled up. 'I don't understand.'

'It's not difficult.' He tugged her down again, pressed a warm, lingering kiss to her midriff. 'You work for me now.'

'But you're leaving.'

'No.' He smiled at her bewildered expression. 'One day, perhaps. Perhaps not. But definitely not until I have to. Not without you.'

'But, James. . .?'

'I'll keep an interest in the practice.' He stroked her thigh. 'If it becomes impossible to stay here—or if we're no longer needed here—it might be useful. But the surgeon who took over has done a good job. He was as keen to stay as I was to have him continue.'

'The hospital?'

'Has already filled my position.'

'And your house? Your beautiful car?'

He laughed. 'Don't seem very important right now.' He dragged his mouth across her skin, lingering at the junction of her thighs. 'What's wrong? Don't you want me to be your boss?'

'It's not that.' And it wasn't. Who was technically in charge didn't make a scrap of difference—they worked as a team here. But what did he mean—he wasn't leaving? Almost frantic now, she wriggled free and knelt to face him. 'I want you here, of course. I love you, you know that. I need you. We all need you. But. . .but I still don't understand.'

'Understand that I'm staying.' His mouth quirked, as if her consternation amused him. 'And understand that you'll have to start behaving yourself.' He touched her scar. 'Any more stunts like this and you'll find yourself out of a job.'

'James, this is an enormous decision,' she protested. 'You don't seem to be taking it very seriously. You—'

'Know what I'm doing,' he said deeply. He was laughing as he pulled her back into his arms. 'Calm down, Tessa.'

'But how. . .? I don't understand. This is so sudden.'

'Only to you,' he murmured, his mouth at her ear. 'I've been thinking about it myself for a long time. Seeing you wounded and bleeding finally brought it home to me that I didn't want to leave, but even before that I'd begun to wonder if Sadakh would turn out to be my Greece.'

She braced herself on her elbows and shook her head slowly, still bemused.

'Around the time you were in London I had a patient I thought was dying,' he continued, his finger lifting to stroke slowly across the sensitive curve of her mouth. 'A man who'd been fascinated by Greece for much of his life, although he'd never visited it. Unexpectedly he recovered and the first thing he did was fly there. The day before I came here I had a letter from him saying that he and his wife wouldn't be coming back to England again, that he'd found the land of his dreams and for the first time in his life he felt complete.'

Tessa stared at him. 'Sadakh's hardly Greece. It's beautiful, yes, but it's also unstable and violent and—'

'It's *my* Greece,' he told her gently. One warm hand curled around her breast and he nuzzled her forehead. 'No wonder, really. All those bloody letters you wrote,' he added softly. 'Your fascination, your passion, your sense of fulfilment used to prickle at me—made me wonder things about my own life I wasn't sure I wanted to.'

He kissed her, the thumb at her breast brushing gently across her nipple. 'Life in London seems strangely pale compared with this. And I believe in what we're achieving here. I don't want to give that satisfaction up.'

'We're the same,' she said in wonder, wriggling around to face him properly. 'You and me, we're the same. You understand.'

'I think so.' He kissed her again lightly, tenderly. 'I love this. The work. The life. The moon. The mountains. The sky. And you.' He smiled. 'Always you. It was you who brought me here.'

'You wanted to help.'

'And I wanted you.' He stroked her cheek. 'You knew that.'

'Only later.' She remembered that first night when he'd kissed her, and felt herself flushing. 'Not. . .not in London.'

'In London you told me Richard had left,' he said deeply. 'From the way you told me I thought you still had feelings for him, but I knew I couldn't let you slip through my fingers again without even trying. You've haunted me for years, Tessa,' he said quietly, stunning her into silence. 'I told myself that it was sex—just frustrated desire—and that all I needed was to immerse myself in your body until I drove you out of my system. But I was wrong. It went far deeper than that.'

Holding her breath, she touched the hardened evidence of his desire. 'You haven't got me out of your system,' she whispered.

'I never will,' he murmured, capturing her hand. 'I love you, Tessa. I love your passion and your caring and your stubbornness. I love the love you have for the people around you, your love for the mountains and the sky and for this magnificent country. I love everything about you. In some ways I think I probably always have.'

'You never said anything,' she said hoarsely.

'There was Richard. I told myself he was what you wanted. Besides, I knew you—that this was your destiny. And until these last months I thought my life was in London. I fought against recognising how I felt, even after we made love.'

'When I told you I loved you you said you were sorry,' she whispered. 'You said that wasn't meant to happen.'

'At the time I still believed that myself,' he admitted. The corners of his mouth compressed ruefully. 'Or at least I was trying to pretend I did. But seeing you injured nearly killed me. It forced me to acknowledge the truth that I eventually would have come to, anyway. I don't want to live without you and we've wasted too much time already. I love you and I love this place and this work we do. I want to stay here. With you. That makes everything—everything that used to seem so complicated—simple.'

'Oh, James.' Tessa was crying. 'This is like a dream. I can hardly believe it.'

'Believe.' He rolled her over, kissed her tears. 'When can we marry?'

'Whenever you want.' She'd spoken with Richard from London, and their marriage was legally over. But an involuntary hand strayed to her longest scar. 'But you should know,' she said huskily, 'they told me at the hospital that after my injuries there's a possibility I'll never be able to have a baby—'

'Perfect working order,' he murmured, sliding her hand away so he could press his mouth to the line. 'Even if the bullets had wreaked havoc that wouldn't change the way I feel but, remember, I've checked personally. There's every chance you'll have our child, if that's what you want.'

'I think I do.' It was a dream she hadn't allowed herself until then, and she laughed her delight and relief, touching his mouth with the pad of her thumb. 'One day. When things are settled. Safe. Is that. . .all right?'

His eyes darkened. 'Yes, it's all right,' he growled, coming up to possess her mouth. 'I adore you, Tessa. If we have children I'll adore them, too. But first. . .' his mouth lowered to her breast '. . .some practice. Hmm?'

'Yes.' She let him tip her back into the pillows. 'Please.'

Next time she woke it was dark. She sat up, sniffed, then nudged him gently awake. 'James,' she whispered. 'Smell. Axel's Finnish chicken Maryland. We should get up.'

'God, no.' He groaned and rolled over, but she prodded him, giggling.

'He's gone to so much trouble,' she insisted, trying to push him from the bed. 'We can't just not eat it.'

'I forgot.' Suddenly he sat up. It was too dark to make out his face but his voice was strained and serious. 'Tessa, there's bad news. I didn't want to tell you before you were properly settled in.'

Tessa stiffened. 'What?'

'Our new paediatrician, your locum, the one you haven't met yet. . .'

'What? What's happened to him?'

'It's not what's happened, it's what he's done,' he said grimly.

Tessa clambered on top of him, her hands at his shoulders, and tried to stop their shaking, half panicking. 'What, James? What? Tell me?'

He pulled her down and tumbled her over, shaking, she now realised, with laughter. 'He's eaten all your peanut butter,' he growled. 'Every last jar. The lot. Total. There's no more.'

'Oh, no.' Tessa pounded his shoulders with her fists, barely able to believe it. 'I didn't even bring any,' she cried, her anguish only half-exaggerated. 'I thought I still had six left.'

James was still laughing. He hugged her, kissed her, rocked her against him so she sat above him. 'But it's worse than that.'

'Worse?' She paled, pushing him away with her palm. 'Nothing could be.'

'Axel's made you some,' he said gently. 'His own special recipe. Ground some pistachios and added mystery ingredients. It's supposed to be a surprise but I love you too much to let you go unwarned.'

Tessa groaned. 'If you love me that much, will you help me eat it?'

James's hands drifted to the thighs that straddled him. 'If I can cover you with it.'

'Deal.' She gave him a long, sweetly appreciative kiss full of the confidence his love had given her. 'No wonder,' she whispered, 'no wonder I love you so much.'

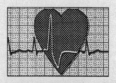

4 FREE

books and a surprise gift!

We would like to take this opportunity to thank you for reading this Mills & Boon® book by offering you the chance to take FOUR more specially selected titles from the Medical Romance™ series absolutely FREE! We're also making this offer to introduce you to the benefits of the Reader Service™—

        ★ FREE home delivery
        ★ FREE gifts and competitions
        ★ FREE monthly newsletter
        ★ Books available before they're in the shops
        ★ Exclusive Reader Service discounts

Accepting these FREE books and gift places you under no obligation to buy, you may cancel at any time, even after receiving your free shipment. Simply complete your details below and return the entire page to the address below. *You don't even need a stamp!*

YES! Please send me 4 free Medical Romance books and a surprise gift. I understand that unless you hear from me, I will receive 4 superb new titles every month for just £2.20 each, postage and packing free. I am under no obligation to purchase any books and may cancel my subscription at any time. The free books and gift will be mine to keep in any case.

M8XE

Ms/Mrs/Miss/Mr..................................Initials ....
                                                                     BLOCK CAPITALS PLEASE

Surname ....

Address ....

....

....Postcode...............................

Send this whole page to:
THE READER SERVICE, FREEPOST, CROYDON, CR9 3WZ
(Eire readers please send coupon to: P.O. BOX 4546, DUBLIN 24.)